BY THE TIGER

RIVERFORD SHIFTERS BOOK FOUR

CRISTINA RAYNE

Fantastical Press

ALSO BY CRISTINA RAYNE

Riverford Shifters

Tempted by the Jaguar

Accepting the Jaguar

Rescued? by the Wolf

Tempted by the Tiger

Tempted by the—Lion?

Suspecting the Lioness *coming Fall 2018

Elven King Series

Shadows Beneath the Falling Snow (A Prequel Story)

Claimed by the Elven King

Date Night: A Bonus Short

Claimed by the Elven Brothers

The Elven Realms

(Sequel series to the Elven King series)

Memories of an Elven Prince

To Love an Elven Prince *coming Summer 2018

Dragon Shifters of Elysia

Where Sleeping Dragons Lie

When Fire Dragons Fall *coming July 2018

The Vampire Underground

Tales from the Vampire Underground Anthology

A Whisper in the Darkness *coming 2018

Incarnations of Myth

Seeking the Oni

Falling for Enma *coming Fall 2018

Fractured Multiverse

(Writing as C.G. Garcia)

The Supreme Moment: Kairos

The Supreme Moment: Externus *coming Fall 2018

Black Crimson *coming 2019

The Golden Mage Trilogy

The Kingdom of Eternal Sorrow

The Man Within the Temple

The Last Stone Cast

Dedicated to all my readers who have journeyed this far with me in this saga. This book would have never been written without all your enthusiasm for the next story!

"*M*axim! Wait! *Please!*"

On any other day, that desperate tone in his little sister's voice would have stopped him cold. However, this wasn't just any day.

This was the day his world had ended.

Maxim Clarke continued through the darkened corridors of his club, Southern Glacier, towards his office at a near sprint, Sasha's voice still crying out to him somewhere behind him. A shudder ran through his entire body as his muscles rippled violently, his body at the verge of shifting. His mind fared no better, his thoughts chaotic with an immeasurable pain and rage and something that was all tiger.

By the time he reached the door to his office, he was barely human enough to have the presence of mind to reach out with a clawed hand to twist the knob, stumble across the threshold, and bolt the door after him. He could sense Sasha only a few steps away from the door; he could sense others not far behind her, but none of that mattered now. He had made it to the place he had come to think of over the last year as his sanctuary.

He was alone. He could finally let go. He could let everything go...

The sound of fabric tearing joined the harsh echoes of his breathing as Maxim felt his body begin to contort and elongate into his tiger form. The grief that had been threatening to suffocate him was instantly pushed aside to the darkest corner of his mind by the pure animalistic rage of a mind that had become nearly a hundred percent tiger.

For the first time since the nightmare of that day in Amarillo had begun, Maxim let out a roar that was so raw, so powerful, that it must have shaken the very building to its foundation. He leaped towards his desk, claws as sharp as new razors extended and attacked everything that sat on the surface—his computer, the stacks of documents that had been placed neatly on one corner, and a couple of picture frames. Pages went flying as he snapped at anything that moved with powerful jaws and shredded everything else that his claws came in contact with as effortlessly as if they were made of tissue paper.

His computer monitor crashed to the ground as he began to slash at the walls like an animal possessed with the fury of hell, roaring and snarling. His mind and vision were nothing more than a sea of red.

Then a cacophony of voices behind him caught his attention, and he immediately turned and charged towards them, slamming into the door with the full weight of his body in his blind fury. He only had time to shake his head violently at the sudden pain that reverberated throughout him before the door crashed open and three large shapes bounded into the room towards him.

With another roar, he attacked before his mind had even registered the burst of both tiger and jaguar scents that had bombarded his senses. He slammed into the side of the smaller of the two tigers and immediately went for its throat with his teeth. However, almost in the same instant, what felt like a sledgehammer slammed into his side, and Maxim went tumbling with a grunt.

Before he could catch his bearings enough to right himself, the scruff of his neck was seized in a pair of powerful jaws, and a heavy weight fell onto the lower half of his body, severely restricting his thrashing hindquarters. He snarled, hissed, and roared even as he felt his body start to go limp in response to the firm grip on the nerves on the back of his neck.

Then between one blink and the next, the smaller tiger came into his field of vision, and Maxim raged at being held helpless in the face of an approaching enemy. The tiger approached slowly, cautiously, its eyes—no, *her* eyes —wide and staring unblinkingly into his own. Maxim stopped struggling and watched the tigress approach, momentarily confused by her non-aggressive behavior.

She stopped and chuffed a couple of times before very deliberately bending her muzzle down to deliver a few affectionate licks to the tip of his nose. Then her whole body began to spasm, and a few seconds later, a naked human girl sat in the tigress's place.

Something deep within the rage and chaos of his mind had stilled as his yellow gaze fixed onto her face. There was something familiar about her scent…

"Maxim," she cooed, looking down at him with eyes full of pain. "Don't do this. This isn't the answer. I'm here. *We're* here. Please come back to us."

Maxim growled, unable to comprehend the sounds coming from the creature before him. A sudden noise at the door had him instantly snarling in that direction. Another girl stood just a step within the room, this one dark-haired and rousing similar feelings of familiarity as the blonde girl sitting calmly before him.

He watched the second girl as she slowly made her way over to the blonde and then just as slowly lowered herself down to sit on her haunches. His eyes followed her as she slowly reached down and picked up a piece of debris from his earlier rampage and handed it to the blonde. The blonde girl instantly stiffened when her gaze fell on the item, and Maxim tensed even more in response.

The two women exchanged a strange look and then the blonde was extending the object in her hand towards him. His first instinct was to swat whatever it was away, but a firming of the jaws at the back of his neck made his attempt weak and pathetic.

"Look at it," the blonde said in that same, soft voice.

Another growl rose up from his throat as Maxim glared at the two, but they both just calmly stared back as still as two statues. Warily, his eyes moved to the item the blonde had extended towards his face.

The moment an image of another young, blonde woman came into focus, his entire being froze. Then a wave of the blackest despair washed over him, and the sound that burst forth from his throat wasn't a growl, a hiss, or even a roar. It was a keening as close to a human

ру stop

scream of emotional agony as a tiger's throat could produce.

A few seconds later, the tone of his cry began to change to something more human along with his body as his tiger soul retreated under the crushing weight of the grief his rage had kept at bay. His mind barely registered that the slightly painful pressure of the jaws clamped on the back of his neck eased, but as soon as he was free, his arms automatically curled inwards in an attempt to move as much into a fetal position as he could with an enormous jaguar still draped across his lower half.

However, that heaviness also soon lifted, to be replaced by the arms of several people lifting him from the ground and then circling tightly around him.

"We're here. We're here," a voice he finally recognized as Sasha's crooned somewhere above his right ear. "For as long as you need, we'll all be here."

Her words, the warmth of his friends and family embracing him tightly only made Maxim sob harder. He wasn't sure even they would be enough to fill the piece of him that had gone with Anna into that cold grave that day.

Today he had buried the woman he loved, and Maxim wished with all his heart he could have died with her.

CHAPTER 1

Maxim stared down at his cell phone, unsure how to feel about the conversation of the past thirty minutes. When he had answered his phone, the last person he had expected the unknown number to belong to was Mitchell Wilson. When was the last time he had even spoken to the cougar shifter? Maybe six months?

He frowned. Understandable, as Mitch preferred to keep his distance from them these days.

"Mother wants to talk to Kylie and Paul."

Almost fifteen months since Karen Wilson dropped off the face of the earth after her betrayal, fifteen months that not even her own son knew where she had gone. She had disappeared in the middle of the night from the safe house the cougars had stashed both her and Mitch the night before Maxim's group had raided the lions' compound of horrors in the Panhandle.

The only message Karen had left was a text sent to the Elders of the Cougar clan begging them to protect her son. No explanations. No apologies. As far as Maxim knew, the only person from Riverford that Karen had spoken to since was Mitch, and even that had only happened two months after she had disappeared.

So why now?

He shook his head. Whatever the reason, the decision to talk to Karen wasn't his to make.

Bringing up his contacts, he selected Hunter's number. It was best not to disturb Kylie while she was in class.

"Hey. Is this a good time to talk?" Maxim asked as soon as Hunter answered.

A pause, then Hunter said, "That sounds ominous."

"That remains to be seen. I just got off the phone with Mitch. It seems Karen wants to talk to both Kylie and Paul."

"It's about damned time," Hunter growled. "I was beginning to wonder if she would ever surface. Is she in Riverford?"

"No, or at least, that's her claim. She wants to set up a video chat."

"Will she be alone?" Hunter asked, a hint of suspicion bleeding into his tone.

"That's the impression Mitch gave me, but I do have to wonder why *now* of all times, especially when she had been so adamant about never having any contact with either Kylie or her father again no matter how often those two have told Mitch that they hold no ill will towards his mother."

Hunter sighed. "It would be great if she only wanted to apologize and clear her conscious, but when are things ever that simple around here? I'm more inclined to believe that the lions are behind this sudden desire to make amends. It *has* been six months since we gained access to the Chicago Alpha's information network thanks to Tori. The bastards may have finally realized that fact."

Maxim felt a growl rise in his throat as it always did at the mention of Nolan Bray's lioness lover, Victoria King. Fifteen months later, and he still couldn't think of a lion without wanting to snarl, even one that had proven herself as invaluable as Nolan's Rogue lioness. He closed his eyes and clenched his jaw until the urge to growl, to rend and tear, abated.

"Speaking of, my people just sent me a couple of thumb drives of data they copied from one of King's European pharmaceutical companies," Maxim said, pleased that his voice didn't betray his momentary inner turmoil. Hunter had enough to worry about right now without adding Maxim's own frequent melancholia to the mix.

"Do me a favor and don't mention them to Kylie just yet," Hunter said. "You know how she is, wanting to do everything herself."

"Not wanting to be a burden," Maxim added dryly. "She may be a Polyshifter, but she certainly picked the right soul as her dominant. A jaguar loner, through and through."

Hunter snorted. "I don't think 'loner' quite describes either of us anymore. It's practically a party in our apartment every weekend as you well know."

"All that noise and comradery is good therapy for all of us," Maxim said quietly.

His gaze fell on the small framed picture of Anna that he kept next to his computer monitor. After the funeral, he had placed that picture on his desk as a punishment for himself, a painful reminder of his failure to save her.

That first day back to Riverford after he had lost her when Maxim had locked himself in his office and had raged in his tiger form was still as fresh in his mind as the day it had happened. It had taken Sasha thrusting the very picture of Anna he was staring at now to bring back his humanity. Afterward, he had sobbed for hours, held in the arms of his siblings as well as both Hunter and Kylie. That had been the first moment that Maxim had allowed himself to truly mourn her, and it certainly wasn't the last.

His smile was bittersweet as he took in Anna's smiling face, her entire being radiating happiness. Captured by his sister's phone in one eternal moment, now, instead of a punishment, he was grateful to have this last, beautiful memento to remember the woman he had loved instead of the horror of the broken body that had succumbed to her injuries before his eyes in the ICU.

"Maxim?"

The sound of Hunter's concerned voice drew him out of his memories. "Don't worry. I'm fine," Maxim assured him.

And he was. Although a part of him had undoubtedly died that terrible day along with Anna, he had known that he had to try to pull himself together, to live, if not for himself, but for the sake of her memory and for the sake of his family and friends. He would not have willingly ever put his loved ones through the agony they had suffered by Anna's death again by giving up.

A sigh sounded through the phone, but instead of the expected admonishment, Hunter said, "Kylie has two hours for lunch today. We'll collect Paul and Ryder and come down to the club around noon. We can order take-out and decide how to go about this new drop in the pond together."

"Sounds like a plan. See you then."

Just as Maxim placed his phone onto the desk, it buzzed twice, signaling an incoming text. Looking down at the screen, his heart clenched painfully when he saw the name above the short message: CALL ME ASAP.

That Nolan Bray had reached out to *him* directly instead of going through his cousin Jack or even Sasha as usual...

Maxim closed his eyes wearily and picked up the phone again. Looks as if that lunchtime meeting would be more interesting than they had thought.

SEEING THE YOUNG, unlikely couple walk into the club made Maxim glad that he could have Arthur and Sasha with him for this first face-to-face with Tori King. He was calm now, but with the way his entire body had tensed at his first whiff of the lioness, he just didn't trust himself to keep control of his tiger. He had warned

Nolan that it could happen, so at least the wolf would be on high alert as well.

He and his siblings were seated at the bar in the center of the large room, Sasha and Arthur on his right acting as a buffer. His eyes tracked them as they slowly approached, holding hands but with Nolan a full step ahead of Tori. Neither one was looking at him, their gazes focused on a point somewhere over Sasha's shoulder.

Good. That meant Nolan had taken his warnings seriously. Although he couldn't bring himself to trust Tori completely, he genuinely didn't want to harm her, either. The goldmine of insider information on the secret workings of the lion clans as well as firsthand knowledge of how a lion assassin worked she had given them went a long way to earning the Riverford and Parker Grove clans' trust. Her father's password, alone, was priceless.

Maxim studied Tori's face with narrowed eyes. Although she wasn't looking directly at him, the lines of her face were completely relaxed, nor was there anything submissive about her demeanor. She walked with long, purposeful strides, her back straight and the hand not intertwined with Nolan's hanging open and loose at her side. Though alert, Tori was not at all acting as though she had just stepped into somewhere she perceived as enemy territory.

In response, Maxim felt some of his tension ease.

"Thanks for seeing us on such short notice," Nolan said, looking at Maxim for the first time.

In contrast to his lioness lover, Nolan was on high alert, his entire being focused on Maxim. Although known as the reckless one within his clan—and maybe rightfully so given he had chosen a *lioness* as a lover— there was little evidence of that right now in the wolf before him.

Maxim slowly extended a hand towards Tori. "Maxim Clarke."

Without batting an eyelid, Tori accepted his hand and gave it a firm shake. "Victoria King. It's nice to finally meet you in person."

He allowed a faint smile to stretch his lips. "Probably long overdue, but we're all here now."

"I'm just sorry that it had to be because of such grim news. Speaking of..." Nolan's eyes swept the entire room before turning to look at the three siblings questioningly.

"Kylie just texted me a few moments ago," Sasha said. "They were waiting for her father to finish up his last appointment before lunch, so they should be along shortly."

Nolan nodded and then reached into the front pocket of his jeans. He pulled out a thumb drive and offered it to Maxim.

"This has everything we discussed over the phone and then some."

"An older encryption was used," Tori added. "That's what caught my attention. The data was from the last couple of months, and yet it was only accessible using a series of passwords the clans last used back when I was still in training."

Maxim stiffened. "That makes me question its validity. It's been six months since we started to hack into the lion clans' servers. If they're doing something out of the norm, something that only *Tori* specifically will notice—"

Tori shook her head. "These were passwords known to only the upper echelons of the clans. I may have been the daughter of the Alpha, but I wasn't an heir. I was only a tool who was expected to follow orders without question. My asshole father had no clue that I even knew them or else he would have immediately changed all of them the moment he realized I had gone Rogue."

"What reason would they have to revert to an older method of encryption?"

"I think it was just an oversight, given that the files that caught my attention weren't actually newer files at all, but older files that had been recently updated. They probably just forgot to update the encryption as well."

"Other than you, we haven't told anyone else about what we found," Nolan said, "and I don't think what's in that thumb drive should go beyond this group at this point—if at all. Bad enough that the lions know about it, but if too many shifter clans free of the lion clans' rule caught wind of it…"

Maxim nodded. "Our strength here in the South lies in the bonds of trust we've established over the years. I can well imagine what introducing that kind of variable into the equation would do to shake that trust."

"Hearing that kind of talk, should you even tell *us* about it?" Sasha asked, pointing at herself and Arthur.

Nolan blinked at her in surprise before turning his gaze back to Maxim. "You didn't tell them?"

"I thought it best for all of us to examine the data together without my coloring the issue," Maxim replied. "Besides, only one of us can truly advise everyone on what the next step needs to be."

"Kylie," Tori said grimly.

CHAPTER 2

*T*he instant Kylie's eyes fell on him and sharpened, Maxim knew he had once again given the game away in either his expression or his overall demeanor. It was almost uncanny how well she could read him, something that even his siblings sometimes had trouble doing. He had often wondered if it was an ability that all Polyshifters possessed or simply unique to Kylie.

After all, being a true Returner, Kylie was unique within a group that was already super unique in the shifter community. However, since it was unlikely that they would ever get to speak to a group of Polyshifters, much less have them as free with their information as Kylie, his curiosity would no doubt remain forever unsatisfied.

Then her gaze fell on Nolan and Tori, and her eyes widened slightly in surprise, then alarm. The Rogue lioness was probably the last person she had expected to see standing behind him.

"Did something happen?" Kylie demanded, her hand squeezing Hunter's more tightly in agitation.

Although her question had been directed to Tori, Maxim answered, "It seems the universe was bored today—or it finally decided to take pity on us and toss another bone. Which one remains to be seen."

"You found something in the data we stole from the lions, didn't you? Something about my mother?" Kylie asked, the hope in her eyes heartbreaking as she looked from Maxim to Tori.

"Not quite," Tori replied carefully. She then frowned and shook her head. "No, it's probably more correct to say what we found *might* or might not have something to do with your mother. Even I don't know enough about the original Polyshifter clans to say *anything* definitively."

Both Kylie and Hunter stiffened at the word "Polyshifter."

Kylie's father, Paul, placed a calming hand on her shoulder. "Perhaps we should discuss this somewhere less open..."

Maxim nodded. "Follow me."

He led their group up to one of the second-floor conference rooms he'd had Sasha and her husband, Erik, set up with sandwiches and other finger foods for everyone. However, with the grave matters they were about to discuss, he wondered if anyone would even have the appetite for lunch.

"I'm sorry Nolan and I have kinda usurped your meeting," Tori said to Kylie as they filed into the room, "especially if what we've found turns out to have nothing to do with your parents."

Kylie shook her head. "Better a wild goose chase than no leads at all."

Maxim watched the two women's interaction with a critical eye. It still bothered him that Tori knew that Kylie was a Polyshifter. Nolan could vouch for the lioness until he was blue in the face, but a part of him would probably always be suspicious of her loyalties. However, it had been Kylie's decision to reveal herself, hoping her candor with Tori would allow them to better examine the mountains of data they were stealing from the lion clans' servers. Even he, the most biased of them all, could see the reason in her argument.

Then his gaze fell on Ryder as the jaguar followed behind Hunter, watching Tori with sharp eyes and nostrils flaring a bit. Given what the older man had been through at the hands of those bastard lions, Maxim wasn't surprised Ryder couldn't altogether hide his agitation from scenting a lion so near.

He knew from Hunter that Ryder always insisted on being present for any conversations Kylie had with either Tori or Nolan. Growing up, Ryder had always played the big brother well to all of them, and now that Kylie and Hunter were practically mated, he watched over Kylie as though she was a blood sister.

Well—that was one thing Maxim shared with the older jaguar. Kylie was now as much a sister to him as Sasha. She had been there one hundred percent for the both of them as they had struggled to pick up the pieces of their shattered lives even though her own heart had been crushed when the cougar named Grace had not been found during the raid.

Sensing eyes on him, Ryder's gaze flitted over to him before he offered Maxim a sheepish grin. Maxim's own lips quirked up as he took a seat at the head of the long conference table. He noted that both Tori and Nolan chose seats on the opposite side of the table as far away from both Ryder and him.

It made him feel both grateful and guilty.

Maxim placed the thumb drive Nolan had given him onto the table, immediately drawing everyone's attention. "Nolan, why don't you start things by telling everyone what you told me over the phone?"

Nolan's eyes immediately fixed on Kylie's group. "There was an anomaly in all the genetics data we've been sifting through for the past week that caught Tori's eye," Nolan said. "A few of the files used an older encryption even though they were dated fairly recently. A boon, really, as we were able to sift through them right then and there rather than have to wait the possible months we've had to with some of the more difficult-to-crack encryptions. What was found, if true, is rather alarming and may finally shed some light on what exactly those fucking bastards were up to in Amarillo."

"More medical files? Pictures?" Kylie interjected.

"It's not so much *what* was in the files that was so alarming as what had been updated—or rather *who*," Tori replied. When it seemed Kylie was about to lunge across the table to wring the answers out of the lioness, she added hastily, "but no, I'm sorry Kylie, none of it mentioned the cougar named Grace at all."

"The files are about Polyshifters."

The room abruptly fell so silent and still that it instantly raised his tiger's hackles, and Maxim was almost unable to keep the growl that had risen in his throat behind his teeth. Nolan was now the center of everyone's attention.

"Me...?" Kylie's question was barely above a whisper.

Nolan shook his head, and the tension that had permeated the room dropped to something a bit less suffocating.

"No. As far as we can tell, your true heritage has never gone beyond those in this room. Not to say that the danger no longer exists. However, if the lions do come for you, it'll be because you're a Returner." He flashed her a pained smile. "Not even Karen Wilson betrayed you that completely."

"I don't see it as a betrayal," Kylie said quietly. "She was just desperate, and it kills me that she and Mitch may still be teetering on that same dangerous ledge, but we'll deal with all of that later. You were saying about Polyshifters...?"

"The digital file, itself, was originally created back in the early nineties," Nolan continued, "but the data contained within spans over a century. There were scans of old letters and pictures—both black and white and color—as well as charcoal sketches of people and places. Hundreds of them. The oldest pencil sketch of a forest scene was dated 1857."

"Surveillance?" Hunter ventured, looking grim. At both Nolan and Tori's nods, he continued, "There have always been rumors of hidden Polyshifter settlements, and Kylie's birthparents prove that there were at least two that had remained hidden until her father's community was destroyed. There's no telling how many others, if any, besides her mother's clan are still out there. They can all be living as humans in the next city over, and we would never know."

His lips curved up into a wry grin. "Hell, I slept with Kylie several times before I found out her true heritage, practically drowning in her scent, and even with the slight variances in her fragrance, the thought of her being a Polyshifter never once crossed my mind. That the file goes back so far without any meaningful hits shouldn't surprise us at all."

"Can you *not* be so blunt about our intimate life in front of my father?" Kylie scolded, her eyes looking sideways at Paul uncomfortably.

Hunter's grin merely widened, looking not at all repentant.

However, Nolan's next words wiped the playfulness from Hunter's expression. "It's not so much the existence of that file that brought us here today but two documents that were among the updated files, dated only last week. The earlier of the two was an email report claiming to have located a couple of Polyshifters in London. The second was the reply to that email instructing the recipient to meet the teams of Sniffers being sent at Heathrow."

Kylie's eyes darted to the thumb drive on the table. "Were there any surveillance pictures?"

"Only one that's fairly recent," Tori replied, "but I'm not sure if it's related as it's dated January 1st of last year. It's a picture of a crowd celebrating New Years at Parliament Square in London. It looks as though it was taken from an elevated position—maybe with a tele-photo lens. There are at least a couple hundred people in the frame but no arrows or circles to indicate a person or persons of interest, so without any other clues, if those two Polyshifters that email mentioned are indeed in that photo, it'll be like looking for a needle in a haystack."

"And to make things especially fun, the report doesn't even reveal the genders or probable ages of the two alleged Polyshifters," Nolan added. "It's a super longshot, but as it's a photo taken in London and Kylie's mother's clan is located somewhere in Great Britain, we thought maybe if Kylie had a look, she might recognize someone, someone she might have seen in old family photos."

Surprisingly, it was Paul that answered. "Unfortu-nately, when the clans sent their children out into the world to attend college, they weren't allowed to bring any personal items that might identify them as 'other' among shifters. But, even if they had, it would not have helped us here. Both Alan and Grace spoke numerous times of the culture shock they experienced when they first left their villages for college. From their descriptions, their communities hadn't changed much in the last few hundred years. Alan's clan had begun to modernize much sooner than Grace's—he, at least, had indoor plumbing, electricity, TVs, etcetera growing up—but cameras? You would think the Polyshifters believed in all that 'capturing one's soul' nonsense as taboo as cameras were to the clan. Grace said the families in her clan would occasionally sit for portraits painted by a local, but other than that..."

"So no family photo albums, gotcha," Tori said with a sigh.

"It's why my mother left her clan without permission," Kylie said. "She had heard stories as a teenager from clan members who had gone out into the world and desperately wanted to experience it for herself. Even though the clan was starting to send a handful of their kids to various colleges in the hope of modernizing, she knew she had no chance of being one of them."

"Because she was the daughter of the golden eagle clan's Alpha," Sasha said with a nod. "I still can't get over the fact that you can shift into a bird and *fly*."

Kylie shrugged. "In theory. Remember, I've never done more than test whether or not I even had an eagle soul. While the thought of flying sounds fun and exciting, I don't like the idea of how vulnerable it would make me—out in the open sky where any hunter with good aim could shoot me down. I'll keep my razor-sharp cat claws rather than talons, thank you."

"I'll second that," Hunter said, leaning over to kiss her affectionately on the forehead. "I suppose I have your father to thank for your jaguar heritage."

"Yes, that's true," Kylie replied with a nod. "My mother never mentioned her Polyshifter community having a jaguar clan, which really doesn't surprise me. I doubt there was any shifter immigration to Great Britain from Central or South America a couple of centuries ago. As far as I know, they only had three cat sub-clans—Siberian tigers, cougars, and Eurasian lynxes."

"A shifter clan with dozens of sub-clans under a single Alpha—just thinking about the politics of that makes my head hurt," Sasha quipped with a shudder.

"It's not so different than the various packs within my own clan," Nolan pointed out.

"Except your pack members all share one family name," Kylie said. "For the Polyshifters, it's very much like the British Aristocracy. One supreme Alpha over everyone, and the Alphas below him or her on the hierarchy equivalent to dukes or duchesses governing over the golden eagle clan, tiger clan, wolf clan, and so on. The sub-clans formed way back when all the unrelated families within the Polyshifter clans chose which dominant soul they would live as for the entirety of their lives because it became necessary for their survival to hide their true heritage from the lions."

"Which explains why they've been able to remain hidden for so long," Maxim said. "They would seem like an ordinary shifter community, especially if some of them lived as humans."

"The human bit was also another strike, besides being the Alpha eagle's daughter, against my mother being chosen to attend a human university. My mom couldn't become dominantly human like my father and me, and those who could were the ones often sent."

"So how in the world did your mother finally manage to persuade them to let her attend a college in the *U.S.* of all places?" Tori asked.

Kylie snorted. "She didn't. She ran away. When she was sixteen, she found out that her father planned to marry her off to the oldest son of a prominent family he wanted to cultivate closer ties with."

"How very Dark Ages of him," Sasha cut in, sounding outraged.

"Yeah. I can't believe arranged marriages are still a thing, but...I really don't know much about her clan's history or society. I was still just a little girl when she told me about them, and very rarely at that. I could tell cutting ties the way she did still weighed on her heavily, so even though I was really curious, I never asked for more details than she, herself, brought up.

"Anyway, Mom ran away, searched out a clansman that had chosen to be one of the few to live with his family outside their village, and begged him to take her in and then to send her to college here in the States. Mom loved American movies and wanted to experience American college life. She never in a million years thought she would run into another Polyshifter over here, much less end up marrying him."

"Do you, at least, know the name of the shifter family that took your mother in? Where they lived?" Ryder abruptly spoke up.

With a start, Maxim realized it was the first time his friend had spoken since their meeting had started. In the past, Ryder had always been a take-charge kind of guy, always the first to offer an opinion. Now, ever since he was released from the hospital, he tended to fade back into the background, eyes never quite losing their wary watchfulness, even when—or *especially* when—among friends and family. To see the man so changed, so guarded, it made Maxim want to punch something or at the very least, roar with all his might if only to relieve some of the fury that always simmered barely beneath the surface of his emotions.

Thankfully oblivious to the silent storm raging in the man at the head of the table, Kylie turned to Ryder and replied, "I only know that his name was Henry, that he was a cougar, and he had married a human. They and their daughter were living in London when Mom joined them."

"Ah—that explains why she chose to live as a cougar," Ryder said.

"Mom said there are very few golden eagle shifters left," Kylie said. "In her clan, at least. Because of this, none of the eagles were ever allowed to permanently leave their village, so she was sure her father had clansmen out looking for her, that he would never stop. She would've stuck out like a sore thumb as an eagle, even here in the States, and she loved being in her cat forms. It was no great hardship when she and Dad decided to live as cougars for the rest of their lives."

"Even without a surname, this Henry is our best chance of finding your mother's clan," Hunter said, his expression suddenly deathly serious. "Just say the word, and we can leave for London tonight."

Kylie's eyes narrowed, and she nodded sharply. "They need to be warned."

Maxim's gaze slid over to Paul, but instead of the

protest he expected, the expression in Kylie's father's eyes just looked resigned.

"I would come with you, but..." Ryder trailed off, looking equally resigned.

"...but one of the Sniffers may recognize either you or your scent," Hunter finished, his expression pained.

"As would I," Maxim said, "but the fewer people poking around London, the better chance of staying under the radar. You especially don't need someone as high profile as me—" He shot Sasha a silencing look as she started to speak. "—*or* my sibs."

Paul sighed, and his lips thinned into a hard line as he looked from Kylie to Hunter. "At least this time, I'll know where you two are going before the fact."

Kylie winced though both jaguars' eyes flashed briefly with old guilt. To say Paul had been less than pleased to find out they had taken Kylie down into the heart of the lions' torture compound with him being none the wiser was a gross understatement.

"As much as I hate the idea of you two leaving the country alone," Paul continued unhappily, "especially somewhere Sniffers are on the hunt for the same people, I have to agree with Maxim. It kills me to stay behind. However, that two jaguars traveling with a much-older human might warrant a closer look is reason enough. Not to mention that my human senses would be pretty much useless helping you to find a single cougar shifter among a city of millions."

Kylie reached over and squeezed Paul's hand comfortingly. "Spring Break starts next week for me, so Hunter and I can use that as our cover for visiting London should anyone ask. I can only hope that Henry is still living in London and that he'll be willing to talk to me at all. That I look so much like my mother may even make him doubly suspicious of me. London may not be under the lions' rule, but all the stories from those who have relatives living in the UK point to them moving more aggressively towards seizing territory within the last couple of years."

"You don't think your mother would have told him about you?" Hunter asked.

She shook her head. "I *know* she didn't. My parents didn't dare risk letting anyone from their pasts besides Paul, Laura, and Karen know of my existence. Remember that the lions had already started to hunt my father as a survivor of his clan's destruction when he met my mother. That's why I'm not so sure she even told Henry about her marriage. 'Hall' wasn't even my father's real last name, and my mother used an alias as well to hide from both her father and the lions. Hell, even my adoption papers are forged. The child of Alan and Grace Hall doesn't exist on paper or electronically."

"But if the cougar the lions were holding captive in Amarillo is indeed your mom, then the lions must know at the very least that she birthed a baby," Tori pointed out.

"And that's why we've never told the jaguar clan Elders my actual history. As long as the threat of a Poly-shifter spy within the Riverford or Parker Grove clans remains, I'll live as a jaguar for the rest of my life." Kylie grimaced. "However, I've known all along that if my parents are still alive and being held captive and if Paul and I managed to rescue them, the only place in the world that would offer them any kind of safety was Mom's hidden clan. Maybe someday, the same will be true for me as much as I hate the thought. I may not have found my parents yet, but I'll be damned if I just stand by and let the lions take that last refuge from us. Plus, if Hunter and I do manage to find them, then maybe I can persuade Mom's family to send some people stateside to help us find her."

Maxim nodded. "In the meantime, all of us can continue sifting through the lions' servers for more clues and keep you posted. I'll arrange for you to take one of my family's planes to Miami and then you can continue on to London from there."

"We can leave at midnight," Hunter said. "That should give us plenty of time to pack and work out an initial 'plan of attack,' so to speak, once Kylie and I arrive in London."

Paul placed a hand firmly onto Kylie's shoulder as she started to rise. "Not so fast," he scolded. "I know you. If I let you leave now, then I doubt you'll remember to eat—" He cast an equally stern look at both Hunter and Ryder. "—any of you. Besides, it would be a shame to let all this good food go to waste."

Instead of protesting like Maxim expected, Kylie merely nodded and settled back down into her chair.

"One more thing," Maxim said as everyone began helping themselves to the food. "I think you two should arrange to meet with Karen tonight right before you leave."

Kylie turned to him with a startled look. She had evidently forgotten Karen was the reason they had all gotten together for lunch in the first place. "What! *Why?*"

"If Karen *is* still compromised and the lions are using her to fish for information, you need to seem as though the status quo still applies. We need to keep the fact that you two are leaving Riverford tonight an absolute secret, and what better way to do that than to call Mitch and set up a video chat with her right now—and keep it."

CHAPTER 3

From the other side of the conference room, Maxim watched with a keen eye his five friends chatting at the same table they had previously sat at hours earlier, only one of them a new edition. If not for the slight stiffness in the usually-mellow Mitch Wilson's shoulders, this could have been a scene from one of their get-togethers at the club or Hunter and Kylie's apartment from any other night, especially with the somewhat muted sound of music resonating in the air from down below.

Mitch sat to Hunter's left, well out of the line of sight of the built-in webcam of the laptop that sat in front of both Kylie and Hunter. Paul and Ryder stood behind them. While his attention was currently on the couple, Mitch's eyes kept flitting over to the laptop's screen that was currently open to a video chat app. Maxim's own eyes glanced across the room at a wall clock. It was finally ten o'clock. Karen should be calling them any minute now.

Hopefully, this call would finally allow everyone present to have some kind of closure—Mitch included. The cougar shouldered far too much of his mother's guilt.

Maxim closed his eyes at the bleak thought. *Like I'm one to chastise anyone about guilt...*

He gave himself a hard, mental shake. Now wasn't the time to get lost in that emotional, dark chasm again. His friends needed him to be at his sharpest right now, to watch and listen for any hints of deception or coercion once Kylie and her family spoke face-to-face with Karen. Although Kylie and Paul knew Karen the best after her son, they were too emotionally invested in the conversation to be anywhere near as objective and observant as they needed to be.

A pulsing ringtone abruptly sounded out, and suddenly the air in the room seemed to thicken twofold. He could literally taste and smell the tension in it from everyone at that table.

It was Paul that reached over to tap the "Accept" button on the screen. When Karen's image appeared, Maxim wasn't at all surprised to see that her face was noticeably thinner than the last time he had seen her over a year ago when he and Hunter had stormed the Wilson house to rescue them from the lioness assassin.

"Hello," Paul said quietly, and Karen's wary eyes immediately fixed on him.

For a long, tense moment, they merely stared at each other. Then Karen blinked, and within that moment, all the energy seemed to drain out of her until it appeared as though even a gentle breeze would knock her over. The tension on their side, however, only seemed to grow.

"I don't deserve it, but thank you for agreeing to talk to me today," Karen said. "I—"

"We don't blame you," Kylie cut in, causing the woman on the computer screen to jerk as if she had just been unexpectedly poked hard in the side. Her eyes widened in something like confusion as her gaze focused on Kylie. "Before you say another word, I just want to stress that. What's done is done and can't be undone. I've made my peace with that long ago. In fact, this meeting isn't for *me* at all, no matter how much you may think so. It's for Mitch and Paul."

Kylie's hand squeezed Hunter's tightly. "It's for *you*," she emphasized firmly.

Karen suddenly looked stricken. "That day you and

Paul were going to run—I was going to take Mitch and run, too."

Mitch flinched, the expression on his face startled. "What!" he all but shouted.

"I'm sorry I never told you this, honey, but I didn't want you to agonize about that, too." Although Karen's answer was for her son, her eyes continued to look straight ahead at the other four. "Two new Sniffers had been initially sent to Riverford to investigate a report by another Sniffer that a Returner had popped up within the Riverford clans—both were cougars—and who better to corner than another cougar, one that they were sure could be threatened."

"Because of Dad," Mitch said with a growl.

Grief and anger flashed briefly in her eyes as the older woman nodded. "That morning, the Sniffers cornered me in the ER practically seconds after I hung up the phone with you, Paul. Even now I'm not sure how much of our conversation they overheard, but they made it very clear that they had and what would happen to Mitch if they even suspected that I was lying to them. However, instead of grilling me about Riverford's new Returner like I had expected, they were more interested in the fact that the man I had been talking to on the phone had mentioned plans for him and someone else to *flee* the city. Their interest was because of something that had just happened in the forest along the southern outskirts of the city."

Karen looked pointedly at Kylie.

"So the Sniffers and that lioness assassin *did* talk to each other before she came for me at your house," Kylie said, her voice flat and showing none of the anxiety Maxim knew Karen's admission must have caused her.

If the Sniffers knew about the assassin tangling with an unknown lion where none was expected, then who else might have been informed? Who else might now be looking for a Rogue lioness hiding within Riverford's clans and in the process, finding *Tori* instead? He would have to warn Nolan as soon as this meeting was over.

"Yes," Karen replied, "but as to how much information was shared between them, your guess is as good as mine. The only thing I was pretty sure of was that neither they nor that assassin had yet uncovered that the Returner they were investigating and the 'Rogue' the lions' assassin was after were one and the same. Because you were with Hunter, they thought you had most likely been given asylum by the Riverford jaguar clan. I—"

She abruptly broke off, and she covered her face with both hands. "I couldn't chance it," she said, her voice thick with emotion and somewhat muffled behind her hands. "I couldn't bear the thought of those bastards torturing Mitch like they did to my Travis before they killed him. I-I told them they were right about the jaguars protecting you and confirmed that we were meeting at my house, that you and Paul were indeed planning on leaving Riverford for good. I agreed to text them the moment we left the house.

"I believe they planned on ambushing our vehicle on the interstate somewhere between here and Dallas. The only thing I could do was send Mitch and his friends to try to locate some of them, warn you that they were there, and then take a gamble that we might somehow lose them by detouring through the backroads. As soon as we parted ways in Dallas, I was going to drive Mitch and me up to Oklahoma and catch a flight in Tulsa. I was forced to betray you to them once. If by some miracle we managed to escape their trap, then I damn well never wanted to be forced into that position again. I figured the best thing was for Mitch to go into hiding in one of our clan's safe houses in another state until our Elders could safely retrieve him while I disappeared from Riverford forever."

"Apparently, their assassin didn't get the memo," Paul said dryly, his hand absently brushing over his side where that very lioness's claws had slashed him open last year.

Karen lowered her hands, her eyes wet with tears and her expression wretched. "That's why I'm not sure how much they were even communicating with each other," she replied, her voice hitching as she visibly struggled to pull herself together, "how many dots they had managed to connect."

"And now?" Paul asked curtly, his entire demeanor radiating tension. "Have they finished connecting them?"

Maxim unconsciously leaned forward a bit, watching Karen's face closely. *Did you betray Kylie more severely than you've admitted? Are you* still *betraying her?*

So far, neither one had mentioned that Kylie was a Polyshifter. While Maxim knew it was very intentional on their side as a precaution against any ears that may be listening off-camera on her side just as he was, there was no way of knowing whether Karen's omission was a sincere effort to protect Kylie's secret from the lions. She could just as well be hoping to trick one of them into confirming a suspicion the enemy may already have in another desperate effort to keep her son safe. Either way, *they* sure as hell wouldn't be the ones to slip up here.

Maxim felt himself stiffen as Karen's expression became impossibly bleaker. "They might have. That's why I wanted to tell you all this right now—not to beg for any forgiveness that I don't deserve or even to come clean. This morning, I saw someone that I'm almost a hundred percent positive is a Sniffer, and I knew this would be my only chance to warn you that something was up."

"There are Sniffers everywhere these da—" Hunter began.

"Where I'm currently staying is not somewhere a Sniffer would appear," Karen interrupted sharply, "unless it's for a very specific reason. If there's even a one percent chance that *I'm* the reason, that they would think me valuable enough to expend any kind of effort to find me... Well, I thought it worth the risk of one final communication before—I'm sorry Mitch, honey— before I cut off communications with *everyone* for good."

Without warning, Mitch shoved Hunter and Kylie over with his entire body until only the cougar's frantic face was captured by the webcam's viewfinder. "Mom! What the hell are you *saying*!"

For the space of a breath, Karen's eyes softened with love, before she closed her eyes and reached a hand towards her computer screen.

"I love you, Mitch," she said firmly before the screen went black and the words "Connection Ended" appeared in the center.

Cursing, Mitch jumped to his feet, only to be instantly stopped by the wall of muscle that was Ryder. Then Hunter was at Mitch's back, grabbing one of the arms that were frantically trying to push Ryder aside tightly.

"What if they're hurting her right now!" Mitch cried as both Hunter and Ryder struggled to keep him from darting to the door.

"We don't know if there were any lions in the room with her in the first place," Maxim said as calmly as he could manage given that his own tiger was as agitated by the display as Mitch likely felt. "She's obviously doing this to protect you most of all. Don't make her sacrifice be in vain by running off and doing something that'll get you killed or worse. I promise you, I'll do everything in my power to bring her home safe if it's at all possible. The best thing you can do to make that happen is to calm down, respect her decision, and do nothing rash or suspicious for the time being."

Mitch slumped within the restrictive embrace of both jaguars, the wild desperation in his eyes melting into pain. "She never told us where she was going. Not me, not even the Elders. At first, I wasn't too worried. I thought like me, she would only lay low for a couple months, give all the clans a chance to identify and drive out most, if not all, of the Sniffers as well as come to terms with all the guilt she was feeling before coming home. Then two months turned into four, then eight, then over a year, and I finally realized that she might not be planning on coming back after all. Over the last few weeks, I've been talking to her a lot. I thought maybe I was *finally* starting to get her to rethink her decision to stay hidden…"

Paul walked up to Mitch and placed both hands onto his shoulders and squeezed firmly. "And we'll drag her back here kicking and screaming if need be, but we *will* find her, Mitch. This has to stop. We can't allow those bastard lions to keep tearing so many families apart. While Kylie and Hunter track down her mother's clan, *we'll* concentrate on finding *your* mother here."

"Or rather, *continue* trying to find your mother," Maxim corrected with a wry smile.

Mitch's gaze immediately fixed on him. "What?"

"I didn't want to tell you until I had something *to* tell, but I figured it would be in everyone's best interest to bring your mother back to Riverford before the lions could sink their claws into her again. We're not about to hang her out to dry just because she was blackmailed into helping them."

"Especially when it's *my* fault that she was backed into such a dangerous corner to begin with," Kylie said firmly, her eyes sad but matter-of-fact.

"It's the *lions'* fault," Maxim corrected before she could say anything else, "and on that note, you and Hunter need to get to the airport. Lana should've already stowed your luggage in my car. Once you get back home, shift and immediately go for your nightly run. Give it about twenty minutes, and Terri and Mark will be waiting for you about a mile down the highway with a change of clothes. Excluding any last minute disasters, I'll already be at the airport to meet you."

Kylie spent a few minutes hugging her father goodbye before turning to hug Mitch while Hunter spoke some last minute words to Paul and shook his hand. She whispered something into Mitch's ear that was too low for Maxim to hear that made some of the tension in the cougar's body lessen before taking Hunter's hand.

"See you in a few," Hunter said as the three jaguars left the conference room, Kylie sandwiched protectively between them.

"Now it's my turn to hold down the fort here," Ryder's voice echoed down the hall.

No doubt the eldest jaguar had meant the words to sound encouraging, but even at a distance, Maxim could hear the tension underlying his words. He looked over at Paul, who was staring longingly at the empty threshold as though itching to run after them. He couldn't help but think that it was good that Ryder had become as close to Paul as Hunter had over the past few months. They would need each other to keep their worry for Kylie and Hunter from eating them up inside.

"He'll take good care of her," Maxim said to the older man.

Paul sighed and turned away from the door to face him. "That's what I'm afraid of," he admitted. "I have no doubt Hunter would give his life to protect my daughter. I only hope that fact won't make either of them reckless, Kylie especially."

He then turned and offered Mitch a hand up. "Come on, son, let's go join Sasha and Arthur for a drink. No doubt we both could use one right now."

"It's probably best I don't call you until I return from Florida," Maxim said to Paul as they all left the room. To Mitch, he added, "Come see me here at the club on Sunday night. We'll go over all the leads on your mother's whereabouts my people have been able to find so far."

Thirty minutes later, he and his wolf security guard, Lana, found themselves hauling several pieces of luggage towards the terminal where his private plane awaited them. It had been at least a month since he'd last had the opportunity to take his plane up, so despite the dire circumstances, he couldn't help but feel a little giddy about getting behind the stick again.

An hour later, Kylie and Hunter joined Lana and him on the plane.

"Any trouble?" Maxim asked over his shoulder as his two friends settled into their seats just behind the pilot and copilot's seats.

"None that we saw," Hunter replied, "or smelled for that matter. Ryder plans on asking a couple of our jaguar neighbors and some of our bobcat friends to help patrol our patch of the forest after a day or so. If anyone asks, he'll tell them that Kylie and I went to the Keys for Spring Break."

"Now *that* sounds like a good time," Lana piped in with a grin. "Sunshine and running through the surf all day. Too bad you'll have to settle for gloomy skies and likely the Tube, instead."

"Maybe someday we can all go," Kylie said with a touch of wistfulness before shaking her head. "No use dwelling on what can't be helped. At least I'll finally get to visit London, even if there'll be no time to soak in all the sights this time. My mother used to tell me stories of all the places she visited while living with Henry's family."

"Speaking of, I didn't give you a chance to give you this back at the club," Maxim said, nodding towards Lana.

She immediately handed a sheet of paper with a list of names and other information to Kylie.

"I don't know how you ever find time to sleep," Kylie joked after both Hunter and she had scanned the list and realized the information he was handing them.

"Although those names are the best candidates for your mother's foster family, you should also take them with a grain of salt. I imagine, as a Polyshifter, Henry would keep a low profile. You might have better luck trying to locate his human wife, instead."

"At least it's a great place to start," Hunter said.

a knock on his office door had Maxim looking up from the text he was reading. A deep inhale through his nose revealed the person on the other side of the door as Paul.

"Come in," he called, then added before the older man could close the door, "I was just about to call you."

The expression on Paul's face went from polite friendliness to alert with anxiety. "You've heard from them?"

Maxim's chest tightened. "I'm sorry, but no. I was going to ask you the same thing."

"Damn it, it's been two weeks to the hour since I last spoke to her," Paul stated, not even trying to hide the worry bleeding into his voice. "I had hoped today…"

He ran his hand nervously through his hair and sat down in one of the chairs in front of Maxim's desk.

"I know yesterday we discussed some of the more likely reasons why neither one of them couldn't check in," Maxim said, "but this has gone on long enough. I've already spoken with Sasha and Arthur, and they agree that I should head to London no later than tonight. I can stay with my uncle and his family and conduct my investigation with their help."

Paul leaned forward eagerly. "I'll clear my schedule. Just give me an hour, and I—"

"Paul," Maxim interjected patiently, "you're the last person I dare risk on what could very well end up as a rescue mission. If Kylie and Hunter are indeed in serious trouble, Kylie would never forgive me if you ended up dead on my watch." He fixed the human with a piercing stare. "I don't want another death of someone I care about on my soul," he added gravely.

"And Kylie, Hunter, nor your family would ever forgive *me* if I allowed *you* to get hurt or killed while trying to protect mine," Paul insisted stubbornly without batting an eye. "That's my daughter and future son-in-law." Pain flashed briefly in his eyes. "I refuse to allow those lion bastards to take what remains of my family away from me, again."

The tightness in Maxim's chest constricted until it

was almost painful to breathe. "I know, God, do I know, but it's not just for their sake that I want—no, I *need* you to remain behind. It's for Ryder's."

Paul instantly stilled before slumping back into his chair, the expression on his face aging him at least ten years. "Because...he's the one person that absolutely *cannot* be allowed in an area where we know Sniffers and possibly assassins are on the hunt."

"...and once he learns that I'm worried enough about Kylie and Hunter to rush off to England, you're the only one he would likely listen to when we tell him he has to stay behind," Maxim finished apologetically. "I don't say this lightly. If it were my daughter..."

"It's only because I know you love them as much as I do that I'll also do as you say," Paul said.

A burst of a specific scent he had last smelled at Anna's funeral abruptly filled the air until Maxim was all but choking on it and the sudden influx of memories that smell triggered that he had purposely kept buried. Although said calmly, the underlying tension Paul couldn't quite keep from his voice told Maxim just how agonizing agreeing to stay behind had been for the poor man.

His throat still tight with memories best left buried, Maxim could only nod.

"Where is Ryder, by the way?" he asked after a few

minutes of heavy silence and the tightness in his throat had finally started to relax enough for him to get the words out. "I'm shocked he didn't come with you. What he must be thinking right now..."

"I did stop by his apartment before coming here," Paul replied, his voice still a bit thick with emotion. "Unfortunately, he's dealing with a work matter that couldn't be put off. He'll be along shortly."

"To think the lions have reduced me to such a useless state," Ryder said bitterly as he, Paul, and Maxim stood next to his opened car door.

Paul placed a comforting hand on his shoulder. "I know the feeling, son, but we're not as useless as we might think. As long as our eyes are open, we can still help Maxim's people sift through all the data we've stolen from the lions' servers as well as be here to scrutinize anything else Nolan and Tori may think is important right away. It's my hope that we may find a promising clue as to where that cougar named Grace is currently being held, or at the very least, whether or not she really is *our* Grace before Maxim returns with Kylie and Hunter. It would be a great welcome home gift."

"I suppose," Ryder groused as he and Maxim clapped each other on the back briefly.

As tense and angry as he smelled, Maxim knew that if he didn't leave right that instant, not even an army of lions would stop Ryder from heading to England, Sniffers be damned. That was a disaster that had to be avoided at all costs.

He climbed into his car. "I'll call you both the second I touch down at Heathrow."

"Take care of yourself," Paul ordered with narrowed eyes in what Maxim had come to think of as his "father" voice. Maxim nodded, but before he could nod goodbye to Ryder and close the door, Paul grabbed his forearm and squeezed tightly. "I mean it."

Maxim needed no further explanation. Sasha had also had the same concern. He had spent an hour with both her and Arthur alone before coming down to the parking garage with Hunter's family. Sasha had even broken down in tears as she begged him to promise that he wouldn't allow his still-lingering-guilt make him do anything reckless. It was a rare sight to see Sasha in tears, much less begging and meaning it, so he knew just how much she was still agonizing about what had happened after Anna's funeral when he had tried to make the part of him that was "Maxim" disappear completely. Even after all this time, they still feared he would self-destruct at the first opportunity.

He couldn't say they were entirely wrong.

"I will."

After the first couple of hours on the plane, sitting in First Class with only his laptop for company, Maxim longingly wished he was piloting instead of stewing in his thoughts. He had tried to call both Hunter and Kylie's cells three times, but as before none of the calls would connect at all, not even to redirect to voicemail. Texts were unable to be delivered. He didn't think it was a case of losing or damaging their phones—they would've called him regardless. He didn't want to believe that they had been captured by the lions, but in all honesty, that's what he actually feared had happened.

By the time his plane finally landed at Heathrow after nearly ten hours in the air, Maxim was so exhausted that he found himself wobbling on his feet as he exited the plane. He tried to sleep some along the way, but his thoughts had been racing way too much for even a short doze.

His older cousin, William, met him right after he had picked up his luggage from the carousel.

"You look awful, mate," William greeted as he wordlessly took the handle of one of Maxim's suitcases.

"I hate international flights if I'm not the one piloting," Maxim replied with a grimace. "It's been a while, Will. I just wish it wasn't business that brought me here this time."

"Nonsense. We'll have any of you any way we can get, even if you'll only have time to share a cuppa with us occasionally while you're here. How's Sasha and Arthur?"

"Sorry they couldn't come," Maxim said sincerely as they left the terminal. "Things are still a bit crazy stateside."

"I imagine," Will replied drily, showing his worry for the first time. "Well now, let's not keep Father and Mum waiting. We all have *a lot* to catch up on."

CHAPTER 5

*T*he news awaiting Maxim when he finally sat down with his uncle, Thomas, was just as dire as he had feared.

"I cannot imagine that type of commotion *didn't* have something to do with your friends," Thomas said gravely. "It's not every day we see a Bond chase scene reenacted in public outside of a movie shooting."

"If that incident did indeed involve my friends, I just can't believe the lions threw all caution to the wind to pull a stunt like that in broad daylight in a place as public as the London Eye," Maxim said. "It reeks of desperation—or something much worse. Infiltration at some of the higher levels of the human government. Security at the Eye is supposed to be pretty impressive— cameras all around the perimeter, thermal imaging, security guards on duty around the clock, the whole nine yards."

Will abruptly slid his tablet across the table to him. "Here. I found a cell phone video someone took of it. It was obviously shot from someone up in one of the passenger capsules, but maybe you can make more of it than me."

Maxim tapped play and watched two people not much bigger than ants dart through the thick crowds along The Queen's Walk past the Eye, followed closely by a line of four more. He paused the footage and squinted at the couple, but at that height, he couldn't even tell if they were male or female.

Feeling frustrated, he pressed play again and watched the remaining twenty seconds of the clip. Four more people separated themselves from the milling crowd on the walkway and joined the chase from the direction the couple was running, instantly surrounding them until they were backed towards the river's edge. Then maddeningly, the footage ended.

"I've found a few pictures and a couple of other videos though the quality of those videos is worse than that one," Will said in answer to Maxim's unspoken question. "I don't think you'll get any use out of them."

"There's no way in hell those security cameras didn't catch any of that," Maxim said.

"We'd have to get in touch with the security manager to look at any of that footage," Thomas said. "I made some inquiries among the clans as soon as I heard the chase mentioned on the telly, and unfortunately, there aren't any shifters among the control room staff. Too boring, I suppose."

Maxim sighed. "No matter. If the lions have embedded their claws deeper into London society than the London clans have realized, then that footage may have already been destroyed. My time would be better spent playing the part of a tourist and sniffing around the area, as well as trying to find out if the Henry Kylie and Hunter were searching for still lives here in London or is even, in fact, still alive."

Thomas nodded. "William and I will continue to ask around to see if we can locate someone who actually got a decent look at the fleeing couple. You can use your aunt's car while you're here with us."

"Not until he's had a bit of a kip," his aunt, Milly, abruptly said from the door. "He looks utterly knackered."

Maxim looked over his shoulder and couldn't help but grin at Milly's no-nonsense expression. "I own a nightclub. I always look like this in the morning, crisis or not."

"You'll be no use to your missing friends if you keel over," she insisted with a frown.

"I'll be fine."

After receiving a set of keys from his very reluctant aunt, he drove directly to the London Eye and parked in a public lot near the attraction. It was Saturday, so the area was already thick with tourists.

For the next couple of hours, Maxim walked among the crowds, listening to all the hundreds of conversations and speaking with any shifters he happened across. As he had hoped, he overheard several discussions of what had quickly, though unoriginally, become known as "The Chase." However, it seemed the only new information he gleaned from all the chatter was likely all speculation and rumor along the lines of "my cousin's boyfriend's sister was here and..."

Most believed it was simply a very flashy instance of gang violence. Even the few shifters he spoke with believed it was a matter between human gangs, and only one had heard talk that the two people being chased were tourists who had somehow run afoul of them. No one could definitively confirm the gender of the two.

After coming up short in the crowds waiting to ride the Eye, Maxim switched gears and decided to join the streams of people strolling along The Queen's Walk, pretending to watch the various riverboats gliding down the Thames while surreptitiously watching and smelling for anything and anyone suspicious.

Then it hit him as shockingly as an unexpected sledgehammer to the head, nearly causing him to run into a couple of children who had paused in front of him to gawk at the boats. That faint scent intermingled with the various smells of the river, nearby restaurants, and the pedestrians walking by—he knew it as well as his own.

Kylie.

He was so shocked that he stood frozen for at least a couple of minutes before his legs remembered to move again. He walked forward slowly, staring out into the Thames with as casual and just a tad bit vacant expression as possible as though he wasn't actually seeing the beautiful scenery before him but was lost in thought. All the while, he took slow, deep breaths, meticulously examining all the scents entering his nose.

As Maxim walked, Kylie's faint scent became slightly more potent. Four steps later, he was rocked a second time when he picked up an even fainter whiff of *Hunter's* scent. Like a bloodhound, he followed those two scents, his heart pounding almost painfully with both excitement and dread before pausing to dig his cell phone out of his coat pocket as a pretense to allow himself to analyze what he had discovered so far.

The scent of jaguar was strongest here where he stood at the water's edge. He began tapping on his phone's screen as if texting as he walked a bit farther down, and while Kylie's scent began to fade, Hunter's scent became stronger until it abruptly disappeared. He stared hard at the pavement, his nostrils flaring as he suddenly realized why Hunter's scent had been so strong. It wasn't fresh, but that small, dark stain on the ground was unmistakably blood.

His gaze wandered briefly over to the edge where Kylie's scent was the strongest, remembering the cell phone footage of the couple being backed up to the brink of the river before the video had abruptly ended. Had she fallen in? Jumped? Had Hunter? The only thing the blood proved was that either Hunter had been injured in that spot or he had already been wounded, and that's just where the blood had fallen.

It would make sense for them to enter the water where their scent would be completely masked, and maybe they managed to swim to one of the riverboats. He would have to ask Thomas and Will if there had been any stories to that effect within the last three days. It would explain why he couldn't get through to their cells phones if they had been ruined by an unexpected plunge into the river.

But if they did indeed escape, it doesn't explain why they haven't managed to get to a phone to call either Paul or me since.

Maxim frowned down at his phone. Or had they maybe ended up trapped somewhere where getting to a phone was impossible? Dammit, there were just too many what ifs and not nearly enough clues.

He turned on his heel and began retracing his steps back to the car. He needed to talk to his uncle ASAP.

Just as Maxim reached the London Eye, the skin on the back of his neck began to crawl as though he had suddenly entered into the line of sight of a predator. His tiger instantly pushed to the forefront of his mind, and it was all he could do to prevent himself from snarling in warning. Ever since the day he had nearly lost himself completely to his tiger's soul, he'd had some difficulty keeping his human side from being overwhelmed when he either felt a negative emotion strongly or his tiger sensed potential danger nearby.

He didn't dare stop as he made his way through the crowd, trying not to be obvious about sniffing the air or to show his rising alarm in his demeanor. He smelled the usual mixing pot of humans along with the expected wolves, tigers, deer, and bear shifters. Not even a molecule of lion shifter to be found, though he hadn't really expected that one.

Even a few stolen gazes over the mass of people

yielded nothing suspicious. If someone was indeed observing him, they certainly blended well into the crowd.

Earlier, Maxim had been contemplating asking Will or even Thomas to accompany him as he conducted surveillance on the list of Henrys he had given to Kylie and Hunter. Excluding the possibility that the feeling of being watched was simply his own paranoia rearing its ugly head, if someone had already marked him this early in the game, then there was no way he could risk dragging his relatives into his mess any more than he already had.

As he neared the parking lot, Maxim contemplated going to one of the nearby cafes before deciding it would probably be safer to drive around London as though taking in all the sights before going to one of the restaurants for lunch in a hotel deep in the city. Driving around would, at least, give him a chance to talk to his uncle and cousin without having to worry about prying ears.

At least not yet.

CHAPTER 6

Maxim was almost finished with his meal when the feeling of being watched washed through him again. This time, he felt his muscles begin to ripple as his tiger demanded to be dominant. He experienced a moment of real panic when his attempt to stop the first rumblings of a shift from progressing went unheeded, and the spasms throughout his body started to increase as his tiger soul practically roared.

It would *not* be quieted, especially when he sensed several more eyes staring at him. There were a handful of shifters dining at the restaurant. No doubt he was releasing some pretty interesting scents at the moment.

Maxim lowered his head and gritted his teeth. He had to calm. The. Fuck. *Down!*

Maybe it was the panic or maybe it was his sudden anger at himself, but the feeling of being on the verge of shifting abruptly left him from one beat to the next. Maxim took a slow, deep breath before he lifted his hastily abandoned fork and began to eat again as if he hadn't just narrowly avoided the biggest shitstorm in existence.

As the seconds passed, the feeling of being observed lessened until it disappeared altogether. Only then did he dare allow his gaze to sweep the entire room. Nothing stood out as suspicious, but that didn't mean someone like a Sniffer *hadn't* been in the room for the few minutes he had been wrestling his tiger soul back into submission.

He was still waiting for either Thomas or Will to text him back about any possible drama concerning the riverboats the day of The Chase. He had hoped to hear something by the time he finished lunch in order to decide how best to proceed, but if someone was indeed spying on him, he no longer had that luxury.

If either Kylie or Hunter had found Henry, then they would've contacted him or Paul by now. Given the little he had learned along The Queen's Walk, they were either captured or on the run and in hiding without the means to call for help.

Maxim needed to stop trying to identify Grace's

London foster family for the time being and just focus on locating his missing friends. He needed to dig up more information about possible Sniffer movements within London. If he could get some idea of where the large group of Sniffers that had been supposedly sent to London to hunt Polyshifters was based, then he could stalk their movements, see if they were still searching around the London Eye area.

A gruesome image of the dead coyote shifter they had found down in the lions' compound of horrors as well as the even-more-gut-wrenching image of seeing his bleeding fiancé within the protective arms of Kylie's friend, Molly, flashed through his mind. Maxim closed his eyes as a wave of grief rocked him to his core, making him glad that he was still seated or else he would've crumbled to the ground.

If Kylie and Hunter had been captured by those sadistic fuckers...

Five minutes later, he was back in his car on a meandering path back to his uncle's house in order to shake off any potential tails. As much as he hated to admit it, pounding the pavement alone wasn't going to cut it here. He needed Thomas to set up a meeting with the London Siberian tiger Elders to see if they would be willing to share what information they had on recent Sniffer activity with him as well as spread the word to the clans to keep an eye and nose out for any jaguars. There weren't any jaguar clans in Great Britain, so jaguar shifters living within the city as well as tourists were scarce enough that a native might remember an encounter with one.

This way he could keep things safely vague. Maxim was loath to start passing out photos of Hunter and Kylie unless he had no other choice. He didn't want to inadvertently give the lions any information about the couple that might allow them to connect Kylie with Grace or the Polyshifter clan they had been sent to root out.

"I THINK we might have found our first lead," Will said excitedly as he burst into his father's study, causing both Maxim and Thomas to look up simultaneously from the newest grainy picture on Thomas's laptop taken during The Chase the older man had been able to locate.

It was still another few hours before several of the Elders had agreed to meet with Maxim, so he and his family had busied themselves with searching out more amateur footage and pictures, as well as scouring through several social media sites and forums for any mention of the incident. Maxim had actually been shocked at how little usable information they had been able to find. It was all mostly just speculation, jokes, and anger about how the gang activity in London had risen so much within the last decade.

Will and Aunt Milly had offered to split the duties and had begun calling friends to ask if they had recently seen any jaguars and if not, to call if they did.

"One of my friend's sister's uni friends said she saw a jaguar couple eating lunch in a café near the London Eye three days ago. She said she and some friends are at a coffee and sandwich bar near the Thames called Caffè Quattro and that she would be happy to meet with you if you could join them right now."

Maxim was already on his feet. "Of course."

Will held out his phone, screen first. On it was a selfie of a pretty redhead with long, straight hair, green eyes, and a big smile. She could have been anywhere between her late teens or early twenties.

"So you can recognize her in the café," Will said. "Her name is Thea, and she's a Siberian. I sent her a photo of you, as well, but should I accompany you?"

"It's best you aren't seen with me from now on if it can at all be helped," Maxim replied then glance over his shoulder to look pointedly at his uncle. "Any of you. It's just a precaution in case the Sniffers target me. Just send me a text if anyone else calls, and I'll call you back as soon as we finish speaking. I should be back in plenty of time to meet with the Elders."

Forty minutes later, Maxim stood in front of the designated café that was much smaller than he had expected and scanned all the people sitting in the handful of outside tables. After he quickly discerned that none of them was the redhead in the photo, he started to head for the door.

"Maxim," an unfamiliar, female voice abruptly said directly behind him.

He instantly whirled around, a hiss threatening to burst forth from his throat, and then froze when he realized he was looking at the young, redheaded woman from the selfie. Only this time, she wasn't smiling. In fact, the expression in her eyes was alert and wary, as though she expected him to attack.

The sweet smell of a female tiger inundated his senses.

"Thea…?" he asked a bit uncertainly, his eyes briefly darting around her for her friends, but there was no one standing close.

The urge to growl warningly suddenly became nearly overwhelming.

She nodded curtly. "I'm sorry to meet you out here like this, but I wanted to make sure you had come alone. What I have to say is for your ears only."

Maxim's eyes narrowed even as his mind raced. Her accent was strange—definitely British—but spoken in a dialect he couldn't quite place. She was a tiger just as Will had said, but she could very well be one of the lions' Sniffers.

"I see," he replied neutrally, staring back at her with an air of expectancy.

"I was going to meet them here, too," Thea continued as though he hadn't spoken, her eyes locked with his and unblinking, "but unlike you, they never showed."

"Who?"

"Kylie and Hunter."

It was said so matter-of-factly that for a long moment, his brain seemed to freeze. He wanted to grab her arm and demand to know where his friends were. He wanted to glance around to see who might be watching them a little more closely than idle curiosity allowed for, but Maxim did neither of those things.

He simply watched her expression calmly without saying a word, but not only did his silence not rattle her as he had intended, but her eyes hardened as if in challenge or maybe even a bit of irritation. He half-expected her to turn on her heel and stalk off, but she didn't so much as twitch while they continued to stare each other down.

"All right, fine," she finally said, the hardness in her

eyes relaxing into something more bland and business-like, though no less serious. She offered him her hand. "Let's start over. Thea Merrick."

Maxim paused for a couple of seconds before clasping her hand briefly in a firm shake. "Maxim Clarke."

"You have no reason to trust me, especially after the way I went about getting you to meet me here, so I'll offer you this freely—I've been watching you since I saw you sniffing around along The Queen's Walk this morning."

Maxim stilled. All those times he had felt eyes on him—could they all have been Thea?

"There were streams of people on the Walk this morning. What about me in particular caught your interest?"

"Because you stopped in the exact spot Kylie Moore fell into the Thames."

Maxim drew in a sharp breath. "How do you know that name?"

"Again, that's information for your ears only," Thea replied. "We can go into the café and talk in whispers over coffee, or we can go somewhere more private but just as public such as The London Eye. Your choice."

A quick glance over his shoulder showed that the only seats available in the small café were a couple of stools at the wooden bar against the glass storefront. They would be on display like fish in a fishbowl. The thought of being trapped inside what amounted to little more than an oversized, enclosed box for over thirty minutes with a woman he wasn't sure he could trust also didn't sit well with him.

"Or we could go with option number three," Maxim said slowly. "My car is parked in a nearby public lot."

"And where would we go?" Thea asked suspiciously.

"Nowhere. We can just sit inside and talk."

She stared at him silently for a few moments before finally nodding. "Lead the way."

CHAPTER 7

*N*either one said anything until they reached his car and Thea abruptly requested that they both sit in the back. With a shrug of nonchalance that he absolutely didn't feel, Maxim unlocked the door and complied.

"How do you know Kylie's name?" he demanded before Thea could even look in his direction, determined not to allow her to steer the conversation as before.

"We were supposed to meet at Caffè Quattro," Thea said. "When they didn't show, I started to get a bit paranoid. I'd taken the Tube, so I called a couple of friends to come get me. While I was waiting, some people coming into the café were talking about a huge fuss that had happened near the London Eye. The couple said it was a chase scene right out of a movie. A young couple was being chased by a group of four men along The Queen's Walk. Then another four came from the opposite direction eventually surrounding them with the river at their backs. Then people started panicking when the guns came out, and a few shots were fired. The man shoved the woman into the drink before he went down. They gathered him up and disappeared by the time the plod arrived…yes, I thought that might ring a bell."

Maxim had been trying to maintain a neutral expression as she had talked and was not at all pleased that some of his recognition of what she had described must have come to the surface. His usual control was slipping, and he couldn't afford to lose his poker face here.

"Because you were watching me…" he prompted with a raised eyebrow.

Thea nodded. "Don't worry. Your behavior wasn't what made me take a second look at you. It was where you chose to stand—and you were not the first to do so, nor the first I continued to observe."

"And yet, here we are," Maxim said. "*You* were the one to call Will to set up this meeting. What was it about me that made you decide—no *risk*—talking to me, face-to-face?"

"The Clarkes are one of the most well-respected families within the London clans," Thea replied. "Not surprising given that Thomas Clarke is the Siberian tiger clan's archivist. We're here because William confirmed for me that you're a Clarke and you were interested in jaguars within the city."

"You know my uncle's family, and yet your surname, 'Merrick,' isn't familiar at all."

She smiled wryly. "It wouldn't be. I'm not from one of the London clans. I'm only here to attend uni."

"That somewhat explains the accent."

"I haven't lived here long enough for the locals to rub off on me, or so my friends keep telling me," she said with a cheeky grin, momentarily throwing Maxim off balance.

In such a tense and serious exchange, he hadn't expected the mild playfulness. Of course, he knew virtually nothing about her, and as the head of a massive, underground information gathering network, that was a position he didn't often find himself in. It was high time to start filling in the blanks.

"How do you know Kylie and Hunter?" Maxim asked for what seemed the umpteenth time ever since he had met the redhead.

The slight amusement instantly died down within her eyes. "Right. It seems Kylie and Hunter had some questions to ask Henry, the head of the family I currently board with, but I'm guessing that you knew that already."

"Go on," Maxim encouraged, refusing to be baited into revealing anything else even though it was all he could do to keep the sudden questions at the tip of his tongue from bursting forth after hearing *that* name.

Thea's head tilted slightly as she silently regarded him for the space of a couple of breaths. "These days the clans don't need a reason to be suspicious of a stranger, especially a foreign stranger, suddenly calling out of the blue wanting to meet," she said finally. "However, this stranger knew something that Henry just couldn't ignore. A name. I've never seen him as rattled as he was when he showed me the picture of the young, dark-haired woman named Kylie who had called and who I presumed was her mate. I never expected to be just as gobsmacked. Grace—that was the name she had mentioned, and Kylie was practically the spitting image of her! You can bet your arse we wanted to meet them!"

"When did this call take place?"

"Three mornings ago. We were supposed to meet for lunch that very day. I had volunteered to check them out before bringing them to meet Henry. When an hour had passed without even a phone call to explain their tardiness, I got spooked and had my friends bring me back to Henry's.

"A few hours later, Kylie called Henry again from a restaurant in Covent Garden sounding angry and frantic. After confirming that it had indeed been Hunter and her involved in that hubbub down on The Queen's Walk and that Hunter had been taken, my friends and I went to pick her up, but we, too, were jumped just outside the building by around half a dozen humans. To make matters worse, before we managed to chase the thugs off, Kylie was pushed into a parked car in the scuffle and slammed her head hard against the bumper. She was knocked out cold and bleeding pretty badly."

Maxim abruptly leaned towards Thea. "So Kylie's in the hospital? Is that what you're trying to tell me?"

The first thing he had done back home when he had first begun to suspect that his friends were missing was call all the hospitals and had instantly come up dry. He had figured that they were either not at any of them or admitted under an assumed name. He had planned on investigating each of them in person later on that day before Thea had called to set up this meeting.

Thea shook her head. "Humans or not, that we were attacked so soon after The Chase was definitely no coincidence. Henry's wife is a retired nurse, so we thought it safer to bring Kylie home rather than the nearest shifter hospital. Then someone tipped off Henry that a young, blond tiger shifter from an American clan was asking questions about jaguar shifters in London, and you know the rest. I sent someone to watch Thomas Clarke's house before I called William. We wanted to make sure you were actually who you said you were, that you could be trusted. Picture or no picture, I would've left you hanging in the café if my friend had never seen you leave that home."

"I could've been staying at a hotel," Maxim said with a frown.

"That was never a concern," Thea replied. "William told my friend's brother that you were staying at his mum and dad's house. Even if you had been out at the time, William or his dad would've passed along any messages to you. Once I didn't show, you would've eventually gone back to your uncle's house and had William text me again. Your identity would've been confirmed then, and I would've set up another meeting."

Maxim grimaced internally. He would have to have a talk with Will about having a better sense of discretion, but he had bigger concerns at the moment.

"If Kylie has been staying with you for at least the past few days, then the fact she hasn't called me means one of two things." He fixed Thea with a hard stare. "You said she had a head injury. Either that injury is so severe that she has yet to regain consciousness, or you and this Henry are denying her access to a phone."

He expected Thea to flinch away from him in alarm, but she merely met him stare for stare, that same challenging look he had glimpsed outside the café returning to her eyes with a vengeance.

"I believe you."

Maxim blinked, instantly ending the stalemate. "What?"

"I believe you," Thea repeated, the hard look in her eyes softening into something undefinable. "That you are who you say you are. That you really know Kylie and Hunter, why they came to London to search for my guardian, Henry, even though you have yet to admit that you know the reason. It's been quite a while since I've smelled such a strong desire to protect emanate from anyone. My senses are swimming in it, so if you don't mind, can we step out of the car for just a moment so I can get some air?"

Once again utterly thrown off balance, Maxim could only nod curtly as his mind ran the gamut between suspicion and bewilderment. *Guardian?*

True to her word, once out of the car, Thea immediately took a long, deep breath and rubbed at her nose vigorously as though she had an itch she couldn't quite get rid of. Maxim watched her like a hawk, half-convinced that this was a ploy to make a run for it.

Even after all the information she had freely volunteered, he still couldn't quite shake the feeling that the whole purpose of setting up this meeting was to fish for information. Was Kylie truly unconscious and in her and this Henry's care, or had he somehow given her some crucial and damaging bit of information he hadn't even considered?

Looking back, he had shown way too much emotion when Thea had mentioned Kylie being injured. Could that have been the insight she had been fishing for, and if so, for what purpose and for whom? Although he too had smelled the strong desire to protect all around him once the redhead had pointed it out to him, he wasn't quite ready to believe that she was on any of their sides.

"You're right. She still hasn't woken up," Thea said abruptly, turning to look at him across the roof of the car. "We had no idea who to call. All we knew were their names, that they were jaguar shifters, and that they had traveled here from America. She had no purse, no ID, not even a credit card on her. She did have a phone in her pocket, but it was clear the river had rendered it unsalvageable. Although her pulse and blood pressure were stable, Ada—Henry's wife—was worried that she hadn't even stirred once in almost three days. Another day, and we would've been forced to send her to the hospital, no matter the potential danger of another attack. Without knowing why she and her mate were being targeted and by whom, it was something that we really wanted to avoid doing."

"I might be able to help fill in some of those blanks," Maxim said slowly, not bothering to correct her about the mate assumption. It would be true soon enough. "Take me to Kylie, and once I've seen her, then we can sit down with your guardian and have a nice long chat."

She offered him a small smile. "Fair enough."

As they both climbed back into the car, Maxim hoped that he wasn't making the worst mistake of his life.

CHAPTER 8

Thea directed him to the London Borough of Greenwich and a brick, semi-detached home in a quiet, relatively average middle-class neighborhood near a large park. They had barely spoken along the way, mostly just Thea giving him directions as well as a one-time call to Henry to let him know they were coming. The rest of the time was filled with a heavy silence that had him tense and his tiger bristling in irritation.

As luck would have it, Will chose to send him a text as he swung around the building to park in the garage in the back. The whole drive over, he had been contemplating whether or not to try to covertly send his cousin a text with the address of the home, maybe even a picture if he could manage it. Now, he had the perfect excuse to do so openly and to gauge her reaction to it.

Maxim pulled out his cell phone from his coat pocket, frowned down at the screen, and then turned to Thea. "It's my cousin, William, wondering why I haven't called. He's always been a bit of a worrywart. I need to let him know about our little detour and that I may be a while."

To his surprise, Thea merely nodded and said, "Knock yourself out. I've only met William a couple of times, but he did seem the excitable type."

Maxim snorted as he began tapping away a short version of what he was up to and where. "I don't think 'excitable' is quite the right word to describe a history professor."

"A history prof? Really? I don't know why, but I always thought he was a solicitor."

Maxim glanced at her sideways and wasn't surprised to find her studying him with thoughtful, leaf-green eyes.

"What are you studying?" he found himself asking before he could think twice about it, a bit discomfited that he was genuinely curious.

"If I had it my way, I'd be studying film or theater, but I'm supposed to be doing something *useful* and *practical* with my life so computer science it is."

"Practical is overrated," Maxim quipped before he returned his phone into his pocket and opened his car door.

"So what do *you* do?" Thea asked as he followed her to the residence's back door.

"I own a nightclub," he answered honestly.

Based on the strange look she directed at him, he was sure she probably thought he was pulling her leg. The knee-length, charcoal-gray overcoat he currently wore didn't exactly scream someone used to the nightlife. Maybe, like Will, she had thought he was a lawyer or—given how she had observed him sniffing around The Queen's Walk, a private investigator.

However, instead of the influx of questions he had expected, Thea merely nodded and turned back to the door. As she unlocked and opened the door, Maxim heard heavy footsteps quickly approaching. Before either of them could step in, a tall, broad-shouldered man filled the entryway, and the smell of a cougar shifter was added to Thea's sweeter tiger scent. His chestnut-colored hair was generously threaded with strands of silver, and he was clean-shaven. The look in his cobalt-blue eyes, as well as his entire demeanor, was extremely wary.

"This is him?" the older man asked, his nostrils flaring as he openly drew in Maxim's scent.

Thea nodded. "Henry, this is Maxim Clarke. Maxim, this is my guardian, Henry Ithell."

Maxim reached out a hand, wondering if the other shifter would accept it. However, Henry slowly smiled and reached over to clasp his hand in a firm shake.

"So you're one of Charles's boys," he said as he stepped aside for both Maxim and Thea to enter the house.

Maxim blinked in surprise. "You know my father?"

"The cat clans used to socialize more often back when he and your uncle, Thomas, were still in school," Henry said. "I haven't seen Charles in ages, but you didn't come here just to visit an old man your father knew in his youth—nor did your young jaguar friends. Follow me."

He had a million questions, but Maxim held his tongue as he silently followed Henry through the kitchen and to a staircase at the end of a dark hall. That he could faintly smell Kylie's scent in the air from the moment he stepped onto the first step should've made him feel at least a little bit relieved that he had finally found one of his missing friends, that Thea had told him the truth about bringing Kylie to this house. However, along with the familiar scent of a female jaguar was the smell of old blood.

Suddenly, he was back there in that underground lab

of horrors, and the coppery scent of Anna's blood was all he could smell. A tremor went through his entire body as his tiger soul began pushing for dominance, but this very thing had happened to him before—dozens of times since that terrible day in his office when his family and friends had brought him back from the edge of insanity. It took a Herculean effort, but Maxim was able to quickly pull himself together before his two hosts could notice anything was wrong.

They climbed two flights of stairs to a third-floor bedroom. The door was ajar just enough to see that a woman with shoulder-length blonde hair was standing next to the bed with her back to them. Only when Henry had knocked and pushed the door open did Maxim see that she had a pale wrist in one hand, likely checking the person's pulse. Then his eyes fell on the face of the bed's occupant, and a surge of that dangerous, old rage flooded his being as he pushed past Henry and hurried to the bed.

Kylie's face was so pale and gray that she looked like a corpse. If it hadn't been for the slight movement of her chest rising and falling as she breathed and the steady drumming of her heart, he might have even despaired that he had come too late.

"How is she?" Maxim asked the woman, whom he

assumed was Henry's wife, Ada the retired nurse, his voice tight with tension as he stared down at Kylie.

"Her blood pressure is slightly elevated, but her pulse rate and breathing are normal," the woman answered as she gently lowered Kylie's arm to rest on the bed again. "However, her pupils are still dilated, so I'm worried that she may have some brain swelling, especially since she still hasn't woken up. At this point, keeping her here may be even more dangerous than sending her to one of the shifter clinics."

What they needed was Paul. Of all the times for the human to be literally an ocean away. However, Kylie was Paul's daughter, and he, more than Maxim, had the right to decide what should be done in such a dire situation.

Maxim pulled out his phone and began bringing up Paul's profile from his contacts. "Her father's name is Paul Moore, and he's a doctor," he announced, looking at first Ada, then over his shoulder at Henry and Thea before fixing his attention back to Ada. "After I speak with him and let him know the situation, I want you to consult with him. We'll let him decide what should be done."

"For the time being, I would ask that you not reveal to him our names and location," Henry abruptly said.

Maxim turned to look at Henry. He was standing slightly in front of Thea, his body language once again wary as he looked back at Maxim with a hint of challenge.

This wariness, this distrust, none of them really had time to be constantly looked at sideways with suspicion at this point. The clock was running out on the unsuspecting Polyshifter clan Kylie and Hunter had yet to find as well as maybe Kylie, herself. It was time for all of them to put their cards on the table right here and now.

He dismissed his contacts screen and brought up a photo app. After scrolling through and finding the photo he hoped would end this stalemate, Maxim held out the phone, screen first, to Henry.

"Paul and this woman were friends in college."

The look on Henry's face was one who had suddenly seen a ghost, but at the same time, was told that he had won the lottery. His face paled, then reddened, before he lunged forward and snatched Maxim's phone out of his hand.

"Grace..." Henry whispered as though speaking any louder would suddenly make the phone disappear. "*Where* did you get this photo?"

"From Kylie," Maxim replied, watching the old man's expressions like a hawk even as Thea moved closer to peek at the picture. "I only know her by her married name of Grace Hall. She's Kylie's mother."

The last thing he expected was for Thea to rush

forward, grab both his arms in a vise grip, and demand, "Where is she! *Where* is Grace?"

"What?"

"The woman in that photo," Thea continued, her voice rising slightly in pitch in her growing agitation, "it's the same photo taken in America that she sent to Henry years ago. That woman is my aunt, and our family has been looking for her for what feels like forever!"

Maxim grabbed one of Thea's hands and had the back of it pressed against his nose before the tigress could even gasp in alarm. He got in one good inhale before she managed to rip it away, but she was too late. Beneath the delicious smell of a female tiger was the same telltale sweetness of a different kind he had smelled from only one other female—Kylie.

"You're a Polyshifter," Maxim said calmly, his eyes catching suddenly thunderous green eyes, his expression daring her to deny it. "You would have to be if Grace is truly your aunt though I have to say that you look nothing like either of them. An aunt by marriage, then?"

"My mother and Grace are sisters. Grace gets her dark hair from my grandmother," Thea finally said, her tone slightly defensive. "The rest of us are redheads."

"Grace…is she—" Henry began before a surge of emotion choked off his words.

Ada quickly went to his side and slid her arms around him, offering comfort that the sadness in her eyes showed she needed as well. He took a deep breath before trying again.

"Is Grace still alive?"

Maxim looked at them in sympathy. This couple had acted as a kind of surrogate parents to Kylie's mother. He could well imagine the pain of having a child seemingly drop off the face of the earth without warning.

"We don't know," he replied truthfully. "The last time Kylie saw her parents, she was eight, and they were on the run from the lions. They left her with their human friend, Paul Moore, who adopted her. They both have been looking for her parents ever since. Last year, we found a promising lead, but I'll let Kylie discuss it with you if she so chooses. That's not the main reason why she and Hunter came here to London looking for you. Now that I know you're the correct Henry, we'll talk as soon as I call Paul, and he decides the best course of action for Kylie."

CHAPTER 9

"I'll be back shortly," Maxim promised Kylie's silent form as he gave her limp hand an affectionate squeeze.

He then joined Henry and Thea out in the hallway, leaving his friend once again in Ada's care. A sense of *déjà vu* washed over him, but he ruthlessly ignored it. This time *would* be different. This time, there was something *he* could do other than sitting by and watch helplessly as someone he loved faded away before his very eyes. He just needed to keep those devastating memories in the past where they couldn't hurt anyone.

Hunter, Kylie, Paul, and Ryder—they were counting on him to keep it together. At least Paul was on his way to London. Maxim couldn't help but feel relieved that the older man was coming to oversee Kylie's care, especially since he had agreed that Kylie needed to be taken to one of the shifter clinics for an MRI.

If anyone could ensure that Kylie's Polyshifter heritage remained undiscovered, it was that man. Uncle Thomas had also volunteered to act as Paul's shifter liaison, and if necessary, to collaborate the backstory they had concocted of Paul's deceased wife being a jaguar to explain why Kylie had a human father.

"I want us to start this discussion on equal footing, so I freely admit that I know Henry is a Polyshifter from the same clan as Grace," Maxim said as soon as everyone was settled downstairs in the living room.

Henry was in a reading chair next to the couch, and Thea, surprisingly, had opted to sit next to him on the leather sofa.

Maxim fixed his eyes on a startled Henry. "I also know that your wife is truly human and not a Polyshifter who has repressed all of her animal souls."

Henry went rigid. "Kylie should not have told you such secrets. Dare I even ask how many others were told?"

"Relax. Only those in our inner circle, those who absolutely needed to know for various reasons, were taken into her confidence. Not even the Elders of their jaguar clan know that she is a Polyshifter. As I said before, Kylie and Hunter didn't come looking for you just to reconnect with her mother's old roots. It's likely the reason why Kylie and Hunter were attacked near the London Eye and even though the attackers were humans, why Thea and her friends were ambushed while picking up Kylie. We've found evidence that the lions have discovered the identities of at least two Polyshifters here in London."

Both Thea and Henry flinched. "What evidence?" Thea demanded.

Once again, Maxim brought out his cell phone and scrolled through his collection of pictures. "Here," he said, handing the phone to Thea. "This was a photo taken in Parliament Square last year as a crowd celebrated New Year's Eve. We know that at least two people in that group were suspected of being Polyshifters. I obviously haven't had a chance to study it again since we've met, so if neither one of you were in that crowd that night, then maybe you'll recognize someone who was."

"Neither one of us were there," Thea said as she frowned down at the image. "Henry and Ada never go out on New Year's Eve, and I was at a party at a private residence. As for the rest of our clan…"

"I know everyone in my clan who currently resides in London," Henry admitted reluctantly. "A handful like me who have chosen to live outside the clan village, and those, like Thea, who are here attending one of the universities. I can certainly make a few phone calls to warn them to be extra cautious."

"Unfortunately, it's not that simple," Maxim said. "There's a reason Kylie and Hunter were looking for you specifically, Henry, rather than just a Polyshifter. However, all Kylie had was your first name, and she was almost certain that her mother never told you that she had a child in order to protect everyone."

"She didn't," Henry confirmed.

"The resemblance to her mother is uncanny. That's why she felt she needed to come here in person, for you to see, but more importantly, to *smell* her. You, more than anyone, needed to believe that she was Grace's daughter. Because of her mother's stories of how she left her village and ended up in your care, Kylie knew that you still visited your old village on occasion. Even as a Polyshifter herself with relatives in that very village, there was still a huge possibility that you wouldn't be willing, or even allowed, to reveal its location to her. If that had indeed happened, at the very least, *you* would be able to deliver her warning."

Henry stilled. "Warning?" he echoed faintly.

Maxim nodded, his eyes moving to look at his phone still clutched in Thea's hands. "I suppose now it really is irrelevant whether or not you recognize a Polyshifter from your clan within the crowd in that picture. I'm only showing it to you to drive home the fact that the lions' eyes have been drawn to London because of whatever evidence the photographer found in it, and as we speak, there are scores of Sniffers scouring the city for them. They've always suspected that there's been an undiscovered Polyshifter settlement somewhere in the British Isles. Hell, even the Riverford clans have heard the various stories of a few Polyshifter clans still hidden across Europe and maybe even South America."

"Find one or two Polyshifters and there's bound to be more," Thea added softly, "prisoners to point the way for those wankers. The Chase…"

Maxim grimaced. "Probably. Something Hunter and Kylie did must've made those Sniffers suspicious. Maybe they made contact with someone from that photo. Maybe it was talking to *you*, Thea, that set them off. I imagine they thought Hunter and Kylie were Polyshifters, or at the very least, knew who they were, and that's why they were willing to go after them in such a reckless manner so publically. To find a Polyshifter village is like finding the Holy Grail for those bastards. As an added bonus, the London clans would likely just think that the lions are making some sort of move on them. They would never imagine that it was the *Polyshifters* hiding in their midst that they were after –and you *are* hiding your heritage from everyone, aren't you?"

Henry's eyes darted over to Maxim's phone still in Thea's hands before settling on Thea. "Apparently not as well as I had thought."

Thea's eyes narrowed. "I never told Kylie or Hunter that you or I was a Polyshifter," she said defensively. "Nor did Kylie reveal her own Polyshifter heritage to me. It was only when she lay bleeding in my lap in the backseat that we smelled the truth."

"Speaking of," Maxim interjected before a war of words could erupt, "who is the 'we' part of that equation?"

Thea turned to him and flashed him a grateful smile. "Friends from my village, though from a different sub-clan and a year older than me. They're also uni students. I thought maybe they would be in the picture you showed me, but I don't see them. Of course, I'd have to talk to them to be a hundred percent sure."

"Call them and ask," Henry instructed, his expression growing even more troubled. "Now is not the time for loose ends."

Thea let out an involuntary hiss as Maxim's phone suddenly vibrated, signaling an incoming call. Her face reddening, she wordlessly handed him the phone. However, his slight amusement instantly melted into alarm when he saw Paul's name on the screen. He wasn't supposed to call until his plane was an hour from London.

"Call your friends while I take this," Maxim urged her before rising and heading out into the hall as he answered the call. "Paul?"

"Don't be alarmed," Paul said quickly, "but there's been a slight delay over on this end. I just wanted to let you know that I'll be taking a later flight than we discussed."

Kylie's father sounded calm, allowing the tension that had seeped into his shoulders to relax. "That's a relief, even though it was rotten luck to have a flight cancellation today of all days."

Paul sighed. "I'm afraid it wasn't the airline's fault this time. As we feared, Ryder didn't take too kindly to being told he had to remain behind while his brother was in all likelihood taken by the lions and Kylie hurt and unconscious. Arthur and Sasha were still trying to restrain and talk sense into him when I slipped out. I can't guarantee that they'll succeed."

Maxim pinched the bridge of his nose, feeling a headache coming on. "We'll cross that bridge if we have to later. Hopefully, I'll have better news for you tonight when you land."

"We'll find Hunter," Paul said firmly. "Just concentrate on that right now, and you let me and everyone else worry about Kylie from now on. I shouldn't arrive at Heathrow more than a couple of hours later than previously planned."

Henry and Thea were talking in low voices when Maxim reentered the living room. They immediately stopped talking and turned to look at him with studiously neutral expressions. There was a tenseness in the air that hadn't been present earlier. He got the feeling that he had just interrupted an argument rather than a conference of any lingering suspicions about him.

"Everything all right?" Henry asked.

"Just a delay in Kylie's father's flight," Maxim replied as he rejoined Thea on the sofa. "So what's the verdict on your two friends? Were they at Parliament Square that night?"

"No, so Henry will have to call everyone else to find out who was. In the meantime, the guys said they would help us try to find out where Kylie's mate was taken. With all the brouhaha those Sniffers caused during The Chase, *someone* must've seen something useful after they nabbed Hunter."

Henry scowled at her. "Given what Maxim just told us, no Polyshifter should be walking the streets *at all*. It's been days since Kylie's mate was abducted. No doubt he has been made to spill his secrets by now."

Maxim shook his head. "He would die first. Those bastards tortured his older brother for over a year before we were able to rescue him. Hunter would never give them the satisfaction, and the lions wouldn't risk damaging such a potential treasure trove of information —at least in the beginning. This has consistently been their pattern when trying to break their prisoners, and there's no reason to think that'll change now with such a tasty prize within their grasp. That potentially gives us another couple of days to find him before they start to really work him over."

"How do you know all this?" Henry asked warily.

"I make it my business to know," Maxim replied as he stood up. "As such, I have a meeting in an hour with the Elders of London's Siberian clan to discuss recent Sniffer activity. It's a place to start."

"I'll come with you," Thea said firmly, jumping to her feet. Before Henry could do more than open his mouth to protest, she turned defiant green eyes to glare challengingly at her guardian. "The fact that there are countless Sniffers currently roaming the streets of London unchecked concerns more than our new American friends. We need to gather as much information about their movements as we can before either one of us even *thinks* to take these warnings to my grandfather. Plus, at least one of us needs to stay hidden to ensure that a message *can* eventually be delivered, and who do you think our Alpha will be more inclined to take more seriously?"

"Be that as it may, that does *not* mean you need to actually be present to hear that information firsthand," Henry insisted.

"It doesn't," Thea allowed, "but I'm still going."

It was somewhat amusing that neither one thought to ask if he even wanted her to tag along—not that he would turn down an extra set of eyes and ears that had already proven how cunning and stealthy she could be with her surveillance of *him*.

Maxim glanced towards the hall briefly before turning back to the pair who were both glaring at each other so fiercely that he half expected them to suddenly lunge at each other's throat.

"Well then, now that that's settled," he said dryly, "I'll just go up and say goodbye to Kylie before we go."

Without waiting for a reply, he turned on his heel and calmly walked out of the room, all the while feeling two sets of eyes boring into his back.

That was one fight he wanted no part of.

CHAPTER 10

*M*axim endured a full ten minutes of his new companion's narrowed-eyed stare as he drove towards his uncle's house before he caved. He had been waiting to see if she would speak first, but she apparently had more patience than he had anticipated.

"What do you want to know?" he asked without taking his eyes off the road.

"I'm trying to *decide*," Thea corrected, her tone making him look sideways at her briefly.

Though she was frowning, he didn't get the sense that she was frowning at him. Not exactly.

He tried again. If it was one thing he hated, it was awkward silences, especially now that he wasn't always one hundred percent in control of his tiger.

"I really do own a nightclub."

"Huh?" she blurted, the utter bewilderment in her voice making him smile.

"In case you were wondering."

"That wasn't…!" She took a deep breath and let it out noisily. "No, never mind. You're right. I should just tell you. Going to college isn't the real reason why I came to London."

Maxim looked at her sharply. "Do I even want to know why you think this is something I need to know?"

"Because you, Kylie, and Hunter—we all ultimately have the same goal."

"To crush the lions?"

Thea paused. "My goal isn't quite so ambitious," she said finally. "I suppose I should've said we share *one* very important goal. My aunt, Grace."

"Kylie did say her mother believed that her family would never stop looking for her," Maxim said slowly.

He saw Thea nod out of the corner of his eye. "We haven't. I don't know how much you know about Grace's father, my grandfather, our village's Supreme Alpha, but royally pissed doesn't even begin to describe him when she ran away. He's not the type of man to let what he feels was a direct attack on his strength, on his authority to lead the clan, to remain forgotten in the past. I'm just the latest he's sent to try to get Henry to admit that not only was he the one who took in Grace after she ran away, but that he knows exactly where she's currently living. To think that after all this time, it was Grace's own daughter showing up out of the blue that finally made him spill the beans."

"And now that you literally held that very information on your lap, what do you plan to do with it? Since you're being so open and honest with me right now, I'll extend you the same courtesy and warn you that I, nor Kylie's father Paul, won't stand by and allow anyone to force Kylie to go to your village or even to meet someone she doesn't wish to. I don't care if the one demanding it is an Alpha."

"Good."

Maxim glanced at her sideways. He wasn't sure what kind of expression he expected to see on her face, but it wasn't the look of utter relief that shimmered in her eyes.

Then he chuckled and shook his head. "I see now why you were so insistent in accompanying me. You're hoping that because you and Kylie are family, we'll help you the same way Henry helped Grace all those years ago."

Thea nodded earnestly. "It's always been my dream

to live outside the clan, to live in and travel a world I've only experienced through movies. I can't ask Henry to help me like he did Grace. There's still quite a bit of doubt as to whether or not he actually did hide her from the clan, so he hasn't been punished in any way. However, he *will* be blamed if I disappear while under his care. My grandfather would likely use it as an excuse to forbid him from ever stepping foot in the village again. Henry's mother and brother still live there. I don't want to be responsible for separating a family forever, but if I were to make it clear that I tagged along to the States with my cousin, Kylie..."

"You do know that once we managed to find Grace's hidden village, we had planned to ask for her family's help in trying to locate Grace as well as Kylie's biological father, Alan," Maxim said pointedly. "There are simply too many promising leads to follow and not enough hands to pull on all the threads. I don't think bringing you to the States with us would inspire much cooperation."

She snorted. "You would have better luck asking a random shifter off the street to help. You have no idea how backwards my clan is compared to the rest of the world. Excluding the ones we send out to attend uni, a lot of my clansmen wouldn't have the faintest idea how to function in a large, modern city like London, much less in another country. We don't even have landline telephones! Only a few families even own a telly—and that's only because we finally got electricity a decade ago!"

"Let's concentrate on finding Hunter and gathering more intel on this newest influx of Sniffers, first," Maxim said. "Then once Paul arrives and Kylie's on the mend, you can discuss this more with them—unless you plan on keeping your current tiger form as your dominant and it becomes my business as well."

"You do know that Grace's mother was part of the golden eagle clan in our Polyshifter community, right?"

Maxim nodded.

"Golden eagle shifters are pretty rare these days. I only know of two remaining clans other than ours in all of Europe. You can well imagine the attention I would've drawn had I shown up to uni with my eagle soul dominant. Any eagles also in attendance would've known within a day that I didn't belong to either of their clans." Thea suddenly laughed. "My grandfather often butts heads with the Alpha of our village's Siberian tiger clan, so I suppose as a form of rebellion against his draconian rules, I would often run around as a tiger. As a result, I've been wearing my tiger form dominantly for so many years that it's the form I most identify, feel comfortable with. I don't have a jaguar soul like Kylie, so if I do decide to settle in Riverford, then yes, I would like to live as a tiger."

"It seems we'll all have much to talk about once this whole mess is resolved."

They were silent for the rest of the drive. Maxim couldn't help but worry at this new potential problem that had suddenly fallen into his lap. Keeping Kylie's Polyshifter heritage a secret from Riverford's Elders often seemed like a full-time job, in and of itself, for not only Kylie and Hunter but everyone in the know. To add another might just turn out to be the spark that finally ignites that whole powder keg of secrets, and he wasn't sure he had the mental stability yet to deal with all the fallout without accidentally losing control over his tiger soul and ripping out someone's throat.

He was a bit concerned when William met them at the door.

"Are we late?" Maxim asked with a frown.

"No," Will replied, flashing a puzzled look at Thea as she crossed the threshold, "but Dad was hoping to talk to you before the Elders start to arrive. He's in his study."

"You know Thea Merrick, right?" he said as they moved into the living room.

Will looked from Thea to Maxim and back. "We've met a couple of times."

"It's a long story, but she's going to be helping us find Hunter," Maxim explained. "I'll let her fill you in on everything she's comfortable revealing about her role in all of this while I go talk to Thomas."

Thea shot him an irritated look, but instead of protesting, she merely nodded curtly. "Fine."

Maxim's lips twitched in an effort to keep from laughing at her long-suffering expression.

"I won't be long," he promised both of them, hoping that things wouldn't be too awkward between them.

As he walked down the hall, he could hear Will asking about Kylie's condition. Some of his guilt for putting them on the spot lessened. Will had just given Thea an out by talking about a subject that was relatively neutral to both of them but at the same time, important. They would be all right.

However, his remaining guilt melted into alarm when he entered his uncle's study and was greeted by his troubled face.

"We don't have much time left before the first of the Elders arrive," Thomas said without preamble. "I just finished speaking with Nigel, a friend who is also an Elder of the Siberian clan. Apparently, a handful of the Elders of various clans already had a brief, covert meeting to discuss *you*."

"They're suspicious," Maxim said grimly.

Thomas sighed and rubbed his eyes wearily. "A few sense that you are not telling them the whole truth in regards to this sudden influx of Sniffers that they weren't aware of until The Chase was all over the telly and the internet."

Maxim sighed. "Can't say that I blame them. They have to be wondering how someone across the pond knows more about recent movements by the lions within London than their own watchers."

"While our family's reputation has given you the benefit of the doubt for now, I'm not so certain going forth with this meeting is wise, anymore. Nigel says they plan on interrogating you on why Kylie and Hunter were in London to begin with and why the British lion clans are so interested in a pair of jaguars from an American clan that they caused such a public spectacle."

"I hate to put you in a bad spot, Uncle, but maybe it would be better that I leave right now and leave my questions about Sniffer movements within the city for you to ask. I think my presence will only muddy the waters on whatever useful information they may be able to provide. In the meantime, there's another avenue I can begin exploring that could yield—"

The door abruptly swung open, cutting him off, as both Will and Thea burst into the room. "Sorry to interrupt, Dad, but one of Thea's friends just called to report a possible Sniffer sighting."

"I didn't realize you brought Miss Merrick with you," Thomas said.

"She's that 'other avenue' I started to tell you about before the interruption," Maxim replied. "Some of her college friends were keeping an eye out for the Sniffers for us."

"It could be nothing," Thea warned, "but a couple of my mates were riding the Tube, and they overheard a group of wolf shifters with American accents arguing over where they should depart. The wolves ended up getting off near Old Street, and my mates followed them to one of those converted warehouses that rent office space. I'm not so sure it's the type of place they would bring a captive, but it *could* be used as a base of operations. At the very least, it's a place to start looking."

"The lions tend to hide within the fringes of the city," Thomas said. "It chills my blood to think the lions are emboldened enough to conduct their business in central London."

"As Thea said, the wolves may not be Sniffers at all," Maxim interjected. "That being said, I agree that we should check it out. Are your friends still in the area?"

"As far as I know, they're still scoping the place out."

Thomas waved his hand towards the door. "Maxim,

you and Thea should go meet with her friends and allow William and me to make your apologies to the Elders."

"What will you tell them when they inevitably ask about the reasons for Hunter and Kylie's visit?"

Thomas grinned, reminding him uncannily of Sasha. "A partial truth. Did you not mention that Kylie was on holiday from her university?"

Maxim couldn't help but grin as well. "Yes, she was on Spring Break. However, if that doesn't appease them, as a last resort, you can tell them a short version of what happened in Amarillo last year, that Hunter may have been mistaken for his brother. Oh, and speaking of Ryder, Kylie's father and my sibs had some trouble convincing him to stay behind again after he was told about Hunter's abduction, so Kylie's father likely won't arrive until around midnight."

"Perhaps that's for the best. Having a human present during our meeting with the Elders, regardless if that human has a shifter for a daughter, likely would've resulted in them not being so forthcoming with their information. In fact, it would probably be best that Paul is taken directly to Henry Ithell's home from the airport. I have a feeling the Sniffers won't be the only ones the clans will be keeping a closer eye on from now on."

"I'm sorry," Maxim said, his chest tightening with guilt.

Thomas looked at him kindly. "Think nothing of it. It's about time someone did more to stop the lion clans' progression throughout the world rather than just wring their hands about it. I'm prouder than you'll ever know that my nephew is at the forefront of this ancient battle, and we, as your family, will do our part."

CHAPTER 11

*T*hroughout their entire discussion, Maxim had felt Thea's eyes doing their damnedest to bore a hole into the back of his skull, so he wasn't at all surprised that her interrogation began the moment they were alone in his aunt's car.

"What happened in Amarillo?"

Maxim looked at her sideways before he started the ignition. He had expected this particular question, especially.

"Another long story and one best told with at least Henry present—though Ada should probably hear it, too."

Thea stared silently for a long moment, before slowly nodding. "I'll hold you to that." She settled back into her seat, and some of the tension in her shoulders relaxed as she dug out her cell phone from her coat pocket. "I'll call Rory and Edwin and let them know we're on our way. Need directions?"

Maxim shook his head. "I've had business in the Clerkenwell area before. We'll park and join them in their stakeout."

She chuckled. "Stakeout—that sounds so cheesy."

"But no less true though my word of choice would be 'boring.' By the end of the day, you'll probably wish you had stayed home."

"The lions are doing God-only-knows-what to Kylie's mate right now because they came here so selflessly to warn my clan that an attack from the lions was imminent. There's no way in hell that I would cower at home while all you blokes put your lives in danger."

"Don't think of it as cowering," Maxim chided gently. "The Polyshifters never would've remained hidden for this long if you all weren't as secretive and isolated as you are. Kylie's father's clan can attest to that—if any of them are even still alive or free."

Thea sucked in a sharp breath. "So her biological father was killed."

"We don't know. He and Grace have been missing for over a decade now. Their trail has been cold for years—until Amarillo. However, even that thread may turn out to be nothing but a dead end."

"Your uncle was right. You're really fighting hard against the lions."

"I'm fighting for my city, for *Riverford*," Maxim corrected, not at all liking the slight awe he heard in her voice. "I'm not so arrogant or naïve to think that I, and a handful of people that work for me, can take on the lions on a global front. It's all we can do to keep the lions from infiltrating Riverford and its suburb, Parker Grove. No, until the rest of the clans that still remain free from the lions' rule stop burying their heads in the sand about just how powerful those bastards have become, all I can do is offer what little help I can. Then maybe someday it'll be enough to wake everyone up to the danger to unite in a joint strike."

"That sounds like it would be a world war..." Thea trailed off uncomfortably.

"It doesn't have to be," Maxim replied firmly. "We simply have to beat the lions at their own game."

"Is that why you're so willing to help keep the Sniffers from discovering my clan's location? Are you hoping that we'll choose to come out of hiding and fight on your side in this game, this war, out of gratitude? You said so yourself that you were hoping to ask for our help."

"To find *Grace*. Only Grace and only because she's a part of your family. I came to England because I hadn't

119

heard from Kylie or Hunter for over two weeks, *not* to stir the hornets' nest, whether that nest is the lions or the London clans. It had been our hope that Kylie and Hunter would be able to locate Grace's old guardian, Henry, and pass on their warnings without alerting the Sniffers to their presence. Getting help from Grace's clan to aid in our search for Kylie's missing parents would've just been gravy. The main objective was always to warn the Polyshifters of an impending lion invasion."

"And Henry will go to our Alpha with your warnings tomorrow morning."

"Hopefully, my uncle will have more info to send along with him after meeting with the Elders. For us, too. Although I would very much like to believe that Hunter was taken to the same building that your friends followed those wolves to, it's a longshot, at best. At the very least, we can confirm or rule out whether or not the Sniffers are operating so deep within the city."

Thirty minutes later, Maxim entered the Clerkenwell area, and Thea directed him to park in a slot alongside King Square Gardens. It was only a few minutes' walk to Old Street and their rendezvous point with Rory and Edwin. However, once they passed a busy café along the way, Maxim couldn't shake the feeling that they were being watched. He had caught the scent of a few shifters as they walked, but none had been wolves, though admittedly when it came to Sniffers, any shifter was suspect.

He glanced over thoughtfully at the redhead walking beside him. She was watching everything around her with narrowed, keen eyes. Well, everything but *him*, which, after all the staring Thea had done in the car, was a bit odd.

By her own admission, she had spied on him before. He couldn't entirely rule out the possibility that she was continuing to have him watched covertly. Despite all they had talked about and his connection to Kylie, Thea and Henry could still very well have some reservations about his intentions towards her clan of Poly-shifters.

"I never did ask," Maxim spoke suddenly, his eyes fixed on her face, "are Rory and Edwin tigers or something else?"

Thea turned and looked at him quizzically. "Rory is from my village's Siberian tiger clan, and Edwin is from the brown bear clan. Why?"

Hmm...the smell of various shifters he had picked up had definitely included both Siberian and Bengal tigers plus a few different types of bears. He would need to dig deeper.

"Any chance one of them decided to come find us, instead?"

She frowned. "Not unless something's gone wrong—wait, what is it you're not telling me?"

Instead of answering, Maxim took her hand and threaded their fingers together firmly before she could get over her surprise and pull away.

He then leaned in and whispered in her ear, "I'm pretty sure we're being followed, so play along. Smile, giggle, as if I've just told you a joke, and I'll explain."

Although the tension in her shoulders didn't relax, she did squeeze his hand more tightly and leaned closer to him as she giggled like a schoolgirl flirting with the football team captain.

"I don't smell any wolves," he murmured, "but my skin is practically crawling with the weight of at least one pair of hidden eyes. If you're sure it's not your friends, then the last thing we should do is show our new tail exactly why we came here."

"We're about to pass another café in another couple of minutes or so," Thea whispered back, "Let's stop for a cuppa, and I'll text Rory that we might not be able to meet up after all."

Maxim nodded and straightened, allowing Thea to lead him by the hand to a small, charming café with a variety of seating choices from normal tables and chairs to colorful rocking chairs and mismatched sofas and armchairs that wouldn't look out of place in a college student's first apartment. He quickly scanned the place through sight and smell, and although his nose picked up hints of various shifters, the scents were old, overwhelmed by the dominant scent of humans.

They were soon seated at a small table in a back corner with an unobstructed view of the entire room, including the entrance, a pot of steaming tea between them.

"Rory says that none of the wolves they followed have come out of the building. He says they don't mind continuing to watch until one or all of them do come out." She suddenly grinned, and some of the rigidness she'd had in her body since he had unexpectedly grabbed her hand eased. "Edwin says to tell you 'We have snacks.'"

Maxim smiled in turn. "In that case, tell them to please do so and thanks." Once Thea finished her text and he was satisfied that the two young humans that had just entered the café didn't set off any alarm bells within him, he added, "I know you're the one I sensed watching me this morning along The Queen's Walk, but did you also spy on me when I had lunch at a hotel restaurant?"

She shook her head. "I took the Tube this morning. Once you drove off in your car, there was no way I *could* follow you. I was pretty irritated about it, you know. At the time, I thought you might've been one of the thugs that had attacked Kylie and Hunter come back to try to pick up Kylie's trail when she reemerged from the river. I suppose we were lucky the one I was watching turned out to be you and not a Sniffer."

"However, the very fact that you were jumped when picking up Kylie after The Chase tells us that I'm not just paranoid."

Thea regarded him silently for a long moment from over the rim of her teacup. "And yet, you're sitting here as calm as though we're just two friends chatting over tea and not someone with one friend likely in the hands of the lions who might be doing unspeakable things to him and the other lying in a coma in a stranger's house," she said finally.

A slow smile stretched his lips as Maxim casually leaned back into his chair. Suspicion confirmed. It had taken a lot less time than he had expected for her to lay that card onto the table.

"I'm calm because I have to be," he replied gravely, his smile instantly gone, "not because I actually am. The rage is there, the fear for their lives, but trust me, when it comes to those bastards, if I allowed myself to feel even a fraction of that rage, then the Londoners would no longer be gossiping about The Chase. Instead, it would be about the huge, crazed Siberian tiger rampaging through the city."

"Amarillo," Thea said abruptly.

Pain, sharp and as unforgiving as a sudden knife to the heart filled his entire being. For a few, agonizing seconds, he was in the back seat of that SUV with Anna bleeding out as he helplessly held her in his arms before the sound of something cracking broke him out of the haze of despair he had started to fall into. Maxim looked down at the ruined teacup now lying in four pieces in his hands and the tea soaking into the dark material of his slacks and grimaced.

Damn, that was twice in one day that he had nearly lost it. Of course, everyone back home tended to avoid speaking directly about that godforsaken day in his presence, so it really shouldn't have been so surprising that he wasn't as fortified against the gut-wrenching emotions hearing the name of that city invoked as he had thought.

It was only when he placed the broken pieces of the cup onto the table and reached for a napkin that he realized that Thea had yet to say a word. Maxim raised his eyes and found her frozen in her chair looking back at him with wary eyes, but thankfully, he didn't smell any fear coming from her.

Then she blinked and opened her mouth to speak. However, before she could even utter a sound, her cell phone buzzed, the sound amplified by the tabletop where it rested by her right hand, shattering the intensity of the moment. Without taking her eyes off him, Thea snatched it up and glanced at the screen."

"Oh, bloody hell!" she hissed, standing up so abruptly that she accidentally banged her knee loudly on the table, causing every eye in the café to turn to them.

Maxim was instantly on his feet, as well. "What is it?"

"We need to leave *now*," Thea said urgently in a voice too soft for the humans around them to hear. "Rory says five of the wolves just burst out of that converted warehouse at a full sprint, and they're heading this way! It could be a coincidence, but..."

"Right." Maxim threw a few pounds onto the table just as the girl who had served them approached them nervously. "Keep the change," he said as they rushed past her and out the door.

Once outside, Maxim grabbed Thea's hand again and began walking leisurely towards Central Street. "We need to get back to the car. Are Rory and Edwin following them?"

"They didn't say, but probably," Thea replied. "We need to hurry. That warehouse isn't very far away."

They had barely made it to the intersection when a sudden shout of surprise somewhere behind them had Maxim turning to look over his shoulder. He saw a middle-aged man hit the ground as a group of five men dressed similarly in jeans and black, fitted jackets plowed through a small crowd of people walking along the sidewalk and headed straight for them.

Not willing to risk a direct confrontation on the slim chance that they weren't the targets, Maxim took off around the corner at a full sprint, yanking Thea behind him. She pulled her hand from his grip and ran up alongside him, matching his pace.

Maxim could feel his tiger soul trying to push to the forefront of his being, and his muscles began to quiver, his body at the brink of shifting. He viciously beat back his tiger instincts that were threatening to inundate his mind—which is why he was utterly blindsided when a gray wolf slammed into his side just as he reached another intersection.

He grunted with pain as the momentum of the wolf's attack pushed him into a bike rack, and one of the handlebars jabbed him hard in his lower back. He barely got his hands up in enough time to shove the wolf back before the bastard could sink his teeth into his shoulder. Then Thea appeared in his peripheral as the wolf lunged at him, jaws snapping. There was a piercing squeal of pain as her foot connected solidly with the wolf's unprotected side, launching him right into the group of, thankfully, un-shifted wolves that had been hot on their heels.

Only a single man managed to dodge that mass of fur and muscle while the rest went down like bowling pins. The wolf shifter reached out a hand towards Thea and managed to snag a handful of her long hair in his fist before she could react. She let out a cry as her head was brutally yanked back. A snarl burst forth from Maxim's throat as he regained his footing, but it was almost immediately drowned out by the man's shriek as Thea's partially transformed hand mercilessly raked down his face with her now razor-sharp tiger claws, leaving four bloody and vertical slices in its wake. The man instantly released her hair to paw at his bleeding face with both hands.

Movement farther behind that chaotic scene had Maxim tearing his eyes away, worried that it was either more wolves or the police. His eyes narrowed, and his lips drew back in a snarl when he saw two young men dressed in jeans and jackets similar to the others, one blond and the other dark-haired, racing towards them.

Maxim grabbed Thea's arm. "Come on!" he hissed, pivoting to make a run for it again before these newcomers could reach them or the pile of wolves on the ground could untangle themselves.

He was immediately thrown off balance when Thea wrenched her arm out of his grip.

"No—wait!" she commanded, jerking her chin towards the approaching men. "That's Rory and Edwin!"

Kicking himself for not having asked for their physical descriptions earlier, Maxim cursed. "They shouldn't have revealed themselves. Now they'll have a big, neon target on their backs."

A couple of the felled wolves had managed to climb to their feet just as the two running Polyshifters reached them.

"Out of the way, you wankers!" the dark-haired one shouted, barreling into the nearest wolf as brutally as a three-hundred-pound linebacker of pure muscle trying to break a tackle.

Or a bear…

Shaking his head, Maxim and Thea joined her friends as they ran past. "Follow me," he said, increasing his speed until he was at the forefront of their odd group.

They would probably have only a two-minute lead, tops, to reach his car before at least some of that wolf pack were snapping at their heels again, less if the actual shifted wolf Thea had kicked wasn't too injured to resume the chase.

They barely managed to jump into the car and lock the doors before the back, driver's side window shattered. Maxim didn't wait around to find out whether it was a kick from one of the wolves or a bullet that had done it. Within seconds, he peeled out of the parking slot, clipping one of the wolves in the side in the process, but unfortunately, not likely hard enough to do any lasting damage. Once back on the street, he gunned the engine and skidded around the corner, keeping as high of a rate of speed as traffic allowed until he had reached the A501 Inner Ring Road.

Everyone in the car had remained silent and so tense that Maxim was almost choking on it as he had woven—sometimes dangerously—around the traffic on the narrow roads, but the moment he had resumed driving normally on the A501, it seemed everyone started talking at once.

"Is anyone hurt?"

"Where are you going?"

"Blimey, that was some brilliant driving!"

"One at a time!" Maxim cut in loudly. He then sighed heavily and zeroed in on the most important question. "Anyone get cut or shot when the window shattered?"

"One of those wolves jump-kicked the window," the blond replied. "It wasn't a gun, thank the Maker. Oh—I'm Rory by the way."

"Edwin," his companion added with a nod. Then his lips stretched into a wide grin. "That was quite an introduction. I guess we can now safely say that those wolves were indeed a Sniffer cell."

Maxim frowned. "Not quite the way I had hoped we would learn the truth, but yes. 'Sooner or later, Poly-shifters always cause chaos.' That was something Kylie once told me her mother would always say." He laughed. "After the day I've had, I'm starting to believe she was right."

"Call it a clan motto," Thea piped in. "My grandfather was particularly adamant in reminding us, and as much as I hate to agree with the old bugger, he was right to drill it into us."

"Which is why we're going back to Henry's house," Maxim said. "You three need to lay low for at least the next couple of days, or at the very least, never be seen with me in public again. None of you were in that photo I showed you, but we don't need those Sniffers getting any ideas. Thea, can you call Will and fill him in on what happened here as well as pass on the address of that converted warehouse? My uncle should still be talking with the Elders. They're in the best position to send a few of their clansmen right now to keep an eye on the building before the Sniffers decide to move their operations."

"We got a photo of the five wolves as they were leav-ing," Rory said.

"Good. Text it to me, and I'll pass that on, too," Thea said.

"At least we got *something* useful out of that fiasco," Maxim muttered.

"If it's any consolation, I don't think any of those Sniffers knew we were watching them," Rory placated. "They might not move at all."

"Especially if they're holding your jaguar friend prisoner inside," Edwin said bluntly.

Maxim growled as the rage always simmering below the surface of his emotions threatened to break through, but his human and tiger souls were somewhat mollified when Thea placed a comforting hand on his bicep and squeezed.

"We'll find Hunter," she said firmly. "Kylie will wake up, and we'll make sure those bloody lions never find the Polyshifters in that photo *or* my clan's village."

Maxim's hands tightened on the steering wheel until his knuckles turned white. He could only nod curtly, not trusting his voice.

CHAPTER 12

"How is she?" Maxim asked Ada as he took the seat next to Kylie's bed the human woman had just vacated.

Ada's eyes softened with sympathy. "I'm sorry, but nothing's changed," she replied. "The best thing I can report is that her heart rate and blood pressure remain stable."

"It's still a few hours until her father arrives. There isn't much more I can productively do right now until my uncle finishes speaking with all the various Elders, so I'll watch over her while I wait for his call or it's time to pick up Paul from the airport, whichever comes first."

"You look a bit peaky," she fretted. "How long has it been since you've slept?"

"I'll sleep once Paul arrives," Maxim answered, side-stepping her question.

After frowning down at him worriedly for a long, tense moment, she finally sighed and nodded reluctantly. "Don't hesitate to call either Thea or me if you need anything."

The room was unnervingly still after Ada left, the sounds of Kylie's and his own heartbeats and breaths echoing throughout the darkened room more loudly than they should have. With no one but his sleeping friend to witness, Maxim allowed himself to sag back into the chair in exhaustion.

It had been over twenty-four hours since he had last slept, and what made matters worse was all the emotional upheavals he had experienced in the last few hours, not to mention that damnable sense of *déjà vu* sitting at someone's bedside always made him feel since Amarillo. He turned and looked down at Kylie's face, feeling not only helpless but guilty. He should have never let them come to London alone. He shouldn't have let Hunter talk him out of sending a few wolves from his security staff to back them up. He closed his eyes tightly with pain both old and new.

He shouldn't have allowed himself to become so weak.

He didn't know how long he had been staring down at her pale face that was half-concealed beneath a breathing mask over her nose and mouth, willing with his entire being for those eyes to open, to flutter, to do anything. *He couldn't think anymore, couldn't register anything other than Anna's next labored breath and the sound of her thready pulse. His eyes ached in an effort not to blink, afraid he would miss the first signs of her waking up from her coma.*

The hand between his own was so cold, so limp, even though he tried over and over to rub a little warmth into her skin. Please wake up. Please wake up…

Maxim bent down and placed a tender kiss on her brow. "Please Anna," he begged brokenly, but she remained as still and unresponsive as the day she had come out of surgery.

That she had survived the surgery at all had given him a small glimmer of hope, but as the hours had turned into a couple of days then a week, his hope had begun fading along with the tiny bit of life that remained within her. Even a shifter's extraordinary ability to heal had done nothing more than cruelly prolong a life that should not have survived the horrific things done to her. Deep down Maxim knew this, but the part of his soul that loved her desperately refused to give up that last breath of hope.

Just once—just once he wanted to see those chocolate-

brown eyes look back at him, see that he was here with her and she was not alone. Even as that thought flitted through his weary, heartsick mind, Anna released a long, heavy breath that was different than those before it. Maxim unconsciously leaned in closer, sensitive to every minute change in her.

It wasn't until the machine behind him started screaming that he realized that he could no longer feel her pulse beneath the fingers he had pressed against her wrist nor see her breath fog up the breathing mask. It wasn't until a swarm of people came rushing into the room that he realized he was now, in fact, alone and then the machine wasn't the only one that was screaming.

"Maxim! *Maxim!*"

The sound of his name being shouted directly into his face had his eyes flying wide open and his body springing to his feet in the same instance. The first thing he saw as he wildly looked around was the still figure on the bed.

"*No...!*" he moaned like a man dying as he staggered against the chair beside the bed.

It wasn't a dream. She was dead. Anna was *dead...*

Then someone tugged hard on his right arm, and Maxim instinctually turned towards the source with a snarl full of rage and grief. A young woman with hair the color of fire blurred into focus as she reached over to grab onto his other arm.

"It's me. It's Thea!" she cried urgently, squeezing his arms tightly and giving him a couple of rough shakes. "Please wake up!"

Thea?

Then sense came flooding back into his mind as the fog of sleep lifted, and Maxim simultaneously recognized the redhead that had him in her grasp and remembered seeing someone lying unmoving on the bed. He whirled around towards the bed so quickly that Thea lost her grip on his arms.

Instead of untidy, blonde strands framing a face devoid of color, a mass of thick, chestnut hair surrounded the head resting on the white pillow. "Kylie..." he whispered.

Then for one terrifying moment, she appeared *too* still until he saw her chest rise up as she took a breath. The relief he felt was so profound that his legs abruptly gave out on him, and he crumbled to the floor.

Thea let out a cry of distress as she rushed to his side, falling to her knees and reaching over to grasp his shoulders just as all the pain and grief from the past year he had kept locked away came rushing back with all the devastation of a meteor crashing into the earth. The wail that burst forth from his throat sounded inhuman as Maxim curled into himself, his entire being a tangle of all the grief and agony his tiger's rage had been protecting him from all along.

It could have been minutes or hours, he wasn't sure, but gradually Maxim became aware that he was shaking as though he was on the brink of physically shattering and holding on by the skin of his teeth, that he was also surrounded by an inexplicable pressure and warmth. It took what seemed like an impossible effort, but he forced himself to lift up his head, to uncurl his upper body until he was more or less in a seated position. All the while, that soothing warmth and pressure around his upper body moved with him.

Within the unending grief and pain that small comfort allowed some semblance of his sanity to remain, and with it came the shame of knowing what, or rather, *who* was responsible for it.

She was at his back, embracing him tightly from behind. He could feel her arms pressing against his stomach as well as her forehead pressing into the back of his right shoulder. Maxim was at once immensely grateful that he couldn't see her expression. What she must be thinking right now, seeing the man she had entrusted the safety of her clan to fall apart so easily without any clear explanation.

Maxim opened his mouth to speak but then instantly pressed his lips together firmly in frustration when he realized he had no idea what to say, how to salvage this situation. He was so lost in his own head at that moment that the feeling of fingertips suddenly brushing softly across his cheek completely startled him, and he was unable to stop himself from flinching away.

"It's all right to cry, you know," Thea murmured softly into his ear, causing an involuntary shiver to course through his body.

Those caressing fingers paused, and she curved her hand until it was cupping his face gently. It was then that he noticed that he didn't feel any dampness on either his cheeks or even in his eyes. He couldn't remember any sobbing at all, just that one cry that had been wrenched from what seemed like the wellspring of both his souls and then falling into a black hole of grief.

Maxim slowly opened his eyes, and the oak armoire across the room blurred into focus. "That—wouldn't be a good idea," he said quietly, his voice tight with tension.

Thea gave his middle an affectionate squeeze. "That's okay, too."

Suddenly, it was too much—her acceptance, her comfort, her softness pressed into his back along with the heady scent of a female tiger. He had to get up! He had to pull away and leave this room, if only long enough for him to rebuild the emotional barriers that had shattered in that one terrible instant.

"This is my fault. I'm sorry."

Maxim's frantic thoughts stuttered and froze. "What?" he blurted.

"You were obviously having a nightmare when I came in. I shouldn't have shaken you awake."

He grimaced. If only it *had* been just a nightmare.

"It was a memory."

Thea stilled, then the hand cupping his face fell away. "Someone—died?" she hazarded. "The way you looked down at Kylie…"

"Yes," he replied roughly.

Maxim tried to pull away, but that just made her arms tighten around him.

"You shouldn't be alone right now," she said stubbornly. "Not until you've calmed completely down. Your heart is bloody well trying to beat itself out of your chest! You don't have to tell me anything—we don't have to talk at all if that's what you wish—but let's at least get off this floor. Henry stepped out to take Rory and Edwin back to their flat, but Ada's still here. Honestly, I'm surprised she didn't come running when you cried out. Maybe she was outside the house."

If a hole had opened up right that second and swallowed him up, Maxim would have welcomed it. God, he was a mess, and he needed to get it together, damn it!

He reached down and gently, but insistently, tugged her arms away from his body until she took the hint and released him. His entire body felt stiff and weak as he stood up on alarmingly unsteady legs. However, he managed to stumble over to the chair next to Kylie's bed and fall into it instead of face-planting onto the floor.

"What time is it?" Maxim asked as his eyes fixed on Kylie's sleeping face.

Just watching her chest rise and fall peacefully helped to calm his still-racing heart. His tiger, thankfully, remained silent within his psyche, probably still in shock from such a powerful and uncharacteristic onslaught of negative human emotions.

"Probably around a quarter after eight," Thea replied as she placed a second, wooden-backed chair next to Maxim's. When he looked back at her sharply, she smiled apologetically. "You slept through dinner, but we thought it best not to wake you. You didn't even stir when Ada came in to replace Kylie's IV bag. Don't worry. We wouldn't have let you miss picking up Kylie's dad from the airport."

Speaking of, Maxim reached over to pluck his cell phone from the nightstand behind him, concerned he had missed an important call or text during his meltdown. He cursed when he saw about a million texts from Ryder.

"Bad news from your uncle?" Thea asked worriedly.

"No, but maybe from back home."

He scrolled down to the first one. It was essentially a warning that Ryder was currently en route to London, and he was expecting Maxim to come pick him up. Maxim could practically hear the snarl in every word. As he skimmed over the rest—diatribes of indignation for being ignored—he felt an absurd urge to giggle as the weight of yet another potential disaster crashed onto his already fractured shoulders, which meant he was probably still not in his right mind.

"It seems we'll have yet another guest from the States come morning," Maxim said in answer to the question in Thea's eyes.

"Someone from your family or hers?"

"I suppose you could say it's both, given that we're as close as brothers, but Ryder is Hunter's older brother by blood. I had hoped my sibs could convince him to stay behind for his own safety, but—"

"—that's his little brother the lions abducted," Thea finished with a nod.

Maxim sighed. "It's a bit more complicated than that, but he's already on the plane, so there's nothing I can do about it right now."

He continued to scroll through his texts, but there were none from Thomas or Paul. He never expected the meeting with the Elders to go on for so long, so hopefully, it was a good sign that his uncle was getting good information as well as a promise of manpower from them and not the usual stonewalling. It wasn't often he found himself playing the waiting game, but today he found a better appreciation for all the frustration Hunter and Kylie had felt every time they had brought a promising lead to him and had to wait for his people to investigate. He felt worse than useless.

It was still hours until he either got summoned back to the house by Thomas or it was finally time to go collect Paul from the airport. He looked sideways at Thea. No doubt she would remain true to her word about not leaving him to stew alone. They both needed a distraction before she could bring up things that he would rather forget ever happened or they choked on an awkward silence that he could already sense building.

Maxim turned his head and offered her a small smile. "There's something I've been wondering about. You speak an interesting mix of both American and British slang. Although your accent is definitely British, it's spoken in a dialect I don't think I've ever heard before."

Thea shrugged. "I like to watch American movies

and TV shows. A lot. Using American slang is fun, especially back in my village. It irritates the hell out of my grandfather. As for my particular dialect, you won't hear it outside my village. My clansmen who leave the village to attend college tend to explain it away as having lived all over Great Britain as well as other European countries just long enough for our accents to change a bit."

For the next hour, they spoke about frivolous things. Thea recounted several funny incidents that had happened to both students and a couple of professors at her university while he told her about some of the more outrageous things he had witnessed at Southern Glacier. It was as though they both had unconsciously agreed to keep things light and cheerful, and Maxim slowly began to feel more like his usual self.

Later that night, he would go over what happened in the next moment over and over, trying to figure out what exactly had triggered it, if he was to blame because of something he had or hadn't done, or if it was just the universe screwing with him yet again. One moment Maxim was telling her about the various clans that lived in Riverford and the next, Thea's lips were suddenly pressing hard against his own and a blast of female tiger pheromones flooded into his system as he gasped in surprise.

There had been nothing in her body language to

warn him that she was about to pounce, so when her mouthwatering scent shot straight to his brain, he had no defense for it. In the next second, Maxim's hands were tangled in her hair as he roughly pulled her face closer and devoured her lips. It was her turn to gasp as his tongue aggressively pressed against the seam of her lips, allowing it to slip through and slide suggestively along the surface of her own, making her shudder and moan and his member swell with arousal.

It was that moan that finally snapped him out of the frenzy of lust her scent had awakened in him even as they enthusiastically tangled tongues.

What the hell am I doing?

His hands still cradling her head, Maxim gently pushed her head away at the same time as he drew away from her plump, kiss-swollen lips. He then closed his eyes and pressed his forehead gently against Thea's forehead before he could see her expression.

"You deserve someone better than me," he said softly, his voice firm but tinged with regret he couldn't quite hide.

His souls were damaged. This incredible, selfless woman who had held a virtual stranger in her arms as he had fallen apart without question deserved a mate who could give her his heart wholeheartedly, who didn't already have a large piece of it forever lost to death.

He felt Thea stiffen when he drew away and allowed silky, red strands to slip from his fingers as he lowered his hands from her head. When he opened his eyes, Maxim expected those green eyes to blaze brightly with anger, but they were curiously blank as she regarded him silently. Then she pulled back from him completely and offered him a wry smile.

"I 'deserve' nothing," she said firmly.

Then without another word, she stood up and left the room. It wasn't until Maxim heard her footsteps on the stairs that he was able to breathe again. That breath inundated his senses with her delicious fragrance that still lingered strongly in the air, threatening to make him hard again.

Maxim took a shuddering breath and turned to look at their silent, unwitting witness. He took Kylie's hand between his own, but even the heat of his skin against the chill of her own wasn't enough to illicit any kind of response.

Everything was so fucked up.

CHAPTER 13

*D*espite only waiting about ten minutes outside Paul's terminal building, Maxim was relieved when Paul appeared wheeling a single suit- case behind him. He needed the distraction, if only for a few moments. Those ten minutes had given him enough time to brood over his kiss with Thea and her reaction to his rejection soon after.

He couldn't get her parting words out of his head— and if he was completely honest with himself, her heady scent and the softness of her lips. It had been a long while since he had felt his blood surge with anything other than rage, and the guilt he felt because of that was almost as heavy as his grief. He had sworn to live on in honor of Anna's memory, but he had never once thought that life would include any kind of romantic intimacy again. Nor had he wanted it to.

It would have been so easy to blame it on his fragile state of mind after yet another emotional breakdown or even his tiger nature when presented with a strong, beautiful female that was the epitome of what made a great mate, but that was just an excuse. The fact of the matter was that he had enjoyed the kiss; he had enjoyed just sitting there talking with Thea about frivolous things. It was what it was, and he was utterly lost on how to fix things between them without hurting her even more than he already likely had.

"Any trouble?" Maxim asked after the older man had clapped him affectionately on the shoulder in greeting.

"None," Paul replied wearily. "I don't know if I should be ecstatic or suspicious, all things considering. After the day you had, I half-expected to suddenly be apprehended by 'airport security.'"

"Don't feel too relieved yet. I didn't tell you when we last spoke because I didn't want to needlessly worry you, but Ryder's on his way over. He should land around five in the morning."

Paul sighed. "I knew I should've just brought him with me. What about Sasha and Arthur?"

"They're staying put in Riverford, at least for the time being. As for things on this side of the pond, I'll need to drop you off at Henry's after I make introductions. My uncle called while I was on the way to pick you up. He said it couldn't wait until morning, and Kylie shouldn't have to wait for that MRI any longer than absolutely necessary."

Maxim filled Paul in on more of the details he had skirted over during their last hurried conversation as he drove them back to Greenwich. Talking with Paul allowed him to feel more like his usual self as the dynamics between the two tended towards business colleagues that held each other in great esteem rather than the more casual relationship he shared with Kylie. As a result, he was able to take all the confusion and guilt he felt about his last encounter with Thea and lock it up behind his usual barrier of professionalism by the time he and Paul stood within Henry's living room, and he was called to make introductions.

It soon became apparent that all that angst hadn't been necessary at all when Thea's actions towards him were no different than they had been before she had witnessed his meltdown. She even held him back after everyone had been introduced as Henry led them up the stairs to Kylie's room and told him that she would be accompanying him to his uncle's home with that same challenging look in her eyes he had witnessed several times since they had met. He wasn't about to say no, resigning himself to a painfully awkward drive.

Paul wasted no time in going to Kylie's bedside, doctor's bag in hand. Ada followed and began rattling off Kylie's vitals as though they had been working together for years.

While Paul was pulling out various instruments, Maxim said, "I'm heading out. Call me as soon as you arrive at the clinic so that I'll know you all arrived safely. I'll meet you there later on once I finish speaking with my uncle."

"You let me worry about Kylie now," Paul replied, looking back over his shoulder at Maxim briefly, his tone stern. "You go do what you need to do. Find Hunter. With any luck, when she wakes up, his will be the first face she sees. And she *will* wake up."

"Yes, she will," Maxim agreed just as fiercely before nodding politely to Henry and following Thea out of the house.

He thought once they were in the car, Thea would sit with her eyes staring straight ahead and not say a word, at least in the beginning. He should have known better given that she had never behaved as expected.

Before Maxim could turn on the ignition, Thea placed a hand firmly over his, making him instantly freeze in trepidation. "Wait. I need to say this now while you getting distracted won't cause a pileup."

So they were going to have *that* conversation now.

"I feel I should apologize, but I don't know where to even start," he admitted, raking his hand through his hair in agitation.

Thea squeezed his hand firmly. "That's because you don't have anything to apologize for. I kissed you because I wanted to, because I've been attracted to you from almost the beginning. You shouldn't feel responsible for that, for maybe losing control and kissing me back before you even knew how you felt about me."

The smile on her lips was self-deprecating. "Believe me, I was just as surprised as you were to find myself sucking on your bottom lip between words, but my tiger soul must've felt there was something there or else it would've never happened. My human side believes that, too, but I also know it was the absolute worst time for it to have happened. You came here to find your friends, and that's exactly what we're going to do. Then afterward, we'll see what happens."

"And if nothing *can* happen?" he told her truthfully.

Her smile was kind, making his heart contract painfully. "I told you I don't 'deserve' anyone or anything. I only told you what *could* be if it's something you'd like to explore, and if that something happens to be that I found an excellent friend, then that wouldn't be a bad thing at all."

He shook his head. "No, it wouldn't."

By the time they drove up to his uncle's house, that terrible guilt that had been wreaking havoc with both his thoughts and emotions had dissipated back into that initial regret he had felt when he had first pulled away from her. He wasn't sure that was an improvement.

Other than a raised eyebrow when he noticed that Maxim had brought Thea along again, Will said nothing as he ushered them into Thomas's office. His aunt, Milly, was also inside, talking quietly with his uncle. Upon seeing him, Milly scowled and forcibly dragged him over to the chair she had just vacated.

"Still looking much too peaky for my liking. I'll go put on a pot of tea," she huffed before stalking out.

Maxim smiled indulgently at his Aunt's back before turning to Thomas. "I hope your unexpectedly long chat with the Elders was worth it."

"More than I had expected, for certain," Thomas replied. "The most important was that the Elder from the lynx clan sent a couple of their 'specialists' to that converted warehouse on Old Street once most of the occupants left for the day. They were able to disable the security and break in without mishap. Unfortunately, unless there was a hidden chamber on the premises, it appears Hunter was not taken there."

"Because that would've been too easy," Maxim grumbled.

"My clan has agreed to hire a few human detectives to rent office space in that building to keep an eye on our American wolf friends," Thomas continued. "They may still lead us to Hunter, yet. In the meantime, the Elders have provided me with a list, complete with photos, of all the sites within London they suspect the lions have infiltrated. Once again, many of my clansmen have volunteered to look at each of them more closely. I'll text you the file so you can study it more closely at your convenience."

"Any ones, in particular, you think I should look at first?"

Thomas turned around the open laptop in front of him. On the screen was a picture of a glass highrise of what were probably condos.

"This property of owner-occupied flats is in the Battersea area. The building was recently purchased by a human, an American entrepreneur who has ties to a pharmaceutical company owned by the lion Alpha of Boston. The Bengals in that area have also reported that this building, in particular, has seen an unusual influx of new foreign tenants in the past two months. All humans, but what has their fur in a twist is that it doesn't appear as if any of them have families, just dozens of young men that are often seen coming and going in the dead of night."

"You think the lions are starting to recruit *humans* in larger numbers?" Maxim asked slowly. "I hesitate to call them Sniffers, but as something more than extra muscle? Maybe as Retrievers?"

"All of that and much, much more, I'm afraid," Thomas replied grimly. "The Elders believe that this is a new tactic the lions are employing now that their progression into central London has all but stalled. There are simply too many large free clans involved in the most influential and powerful of London's business and financial districts. Using Sniffers and even assassins are no longer as effective in twenty-first century London. Thus, it's thought the lions are beginning to reveal their true natures to certain vetted humans already positioned in or recent college graduates just entering the businesses best able to move their agenda of absolute subjugation forward more quickly."

"Are you sure that these humans are *really* human?" Thea abruptly cut in.

Maxim looked at her sharply, not at all liking the picture he was suddenly seeing. "That's more than possible, disturbingly so."

Both Thomas and Will looked at first him and then Thea with puzzled expressions before Thomas suddenly hissed in understanding. "Polyshifters."

"It's been over twenty years since the lions raided and enslaved Kylie's biological father's Canadian clan," Maxim said. "The ages would be right for the college grads. Polyshifters have always been used to infiltrate free clans in order to expose weaknesses. The next logical step would be to use them to infiltrate the businesses they're targeting rather than starting a new business venture from the ground up, but the problem with this idea is Polyshifters are a rare commodity. Also, the consensus has always been that the lions only had around a couple dozen under their thumb in the entire world. However, depending on how many adults in that raided clan they were able to coerce to follow orders or children young enough to mold into loyal little soldiers, the lions could now have hundreds of Polyshifters to use in their schemes."

"And given it's not known except by perhaps a handful that Polyshifters can repress all of their animal souls and appear purely human, the Elders would never think these new chess pieces anything other than human," Thomas reasoned.

"Let's just keep that between us for the time being," Maxim said. "Right now it would do more damage than good if the clans started to suspect even the humans of being Polyshifters. It's enough that at the very least *you* know, Uncle. When this is all over, you can reveal our suspicions at your discretion. You can even tell them we discovered this 'new' truth during our investigations. That way they won't suspect any of us are Polyshifters. Kylie's been through enough hell over her heritage, and I don't want any of that directed at Thea and Henry."

"Speaking of Polyshifters, have you been able to figure out which two in that photo the lions are targeting?" Will asked just as Milly returned with a tray of tea and strips of homemade jerky, both of which she offered to Maxim, first.

"Thanks," he said gratefully, devouring a strip before answering Will. "No, which is why Henry believes that if there is indeed a Polyshifter or two in the photo, then it's not one from his and Thea's clan. Kylie's father, Alan, escaped the raid on his village. There were probably others that did the same and not just from his doomed clan. That Polyshifter or shifters may have inadvertently endangered the Polyshifter clan that has long been rumored to exist in this area simply by drawing the eyes of the lions to them."

Maxim's phone suddenly vibrated in his pocket, and he immediately dug it out, relieved to see Paul's name on the screen.

"We made it to your uncle's clan's clinic without any trouble," Paul said. "We're prepping Kylie right now for the MRI. Any news on Hunter?"

"Just a dead end and a list of leads I can't start looking into until the morning. Thea and I should be along soon," Maxim said. "Once you get her settled into a private room, text me the number. I have a lot to tell you, and hopefully, by then, you'll have a better grasp on why Kylie hasn't woken up."

CHAPTER 14

*A*s an extra precaution, Maxim took a roundabout way to the clinic, thankful that it had an underground parking garage. The broken window in his aunt's car that they had hastily covered with a piece of cardboard and duct tape stuck out like a sore thumb, but he was loathed to borrow Will's or Thomas's car in case they were attacked again.

Thea filled the silence by picking up the casual conversation they had been enjoying before their tiger instincts had thrown a big fat wrench into everything. She seemed to genuinely enjoy telling him stories about her life as well as grilling him about all things American, and he, in turn, was grateful for the short distraction from the utter helplessness he felt in regards to Kylie and the fear and worry over what those lion fuckers were doing to Hunter.

It was as though that kiss and his rejection of it, of her, had never happened. For the first time, Maxim started to believe that a true friendship could be possible between them. She was as comfortable to talk to as Kylie or Sasha, and just as with them, the black cloud of despair that had taken up permanent residence in his human soul since he had lost Anna seemed to lift, if only for that moment.

However, that bit of lightness talking with Thea had given to his wounded soul instantly disappeared when he entered Kylie's room and saw the worry on Paul's face before the older man could completely hide it. Ada and Henry were also in the room. From their positions standing together in the far corner of the room, it was apparent that the three of them had been talking with their heads together, not wanting to be overheard.

"So what's the verdict?" Maxim asked as he walked over to Kylie's bedside.

The only thing new that he could see was a pulse oximeter on one of her fingers. He was immensely relieved not to see an oxygen mask over her face. He didn't think he would have been able to handle seeing her like that.

"Unfortunately, the MRI only raised more questions," Paul answered, the frustration evident in his voice. "The good news is that we didn't see any bleeding or swelling in her brain. Her initial unconsciousness was likely caused by a concussion. However, it's what we found on the MRI that's probably why she's currently in a coma. Her brain activity's off the chart, something we should *not* see in a coma patient—a human one, anyway."

Maxim frowned. "What do you mean?"

"Working shifts in the jaguar clan's clinic this past year has allowed me to compare and contrast human and shifter physiology, at least in regards to the big cat shifters. I've noticed that in a few specific instances when the shifter suffered a traumatic, mental shock while in their human form that causes them to faint, their animal soul becomes dominant, resulting in a forced shift. Once while I was observing an fMRI scan, this type of shift occurred when an extremely claustrophobic patient had a panic attack and fainted in the middle of the scan. That person's neural activity during the shift and Kylie's look the same."

"Are you trying to say that Kylie's unconsciously trying to shift and—can't?" Maxim asked incredulously. "That's why she's unconscious? I sat with her for hours and never once saw her muscles ripple or even her heart rate speed up."

Paul shook his head. "Not quite. It's possible that splitting her head open and losing consciousness in that traumatic moment unleashed *all* her various animal souls at once, and it's that fight for dominance against her jaguar soul without a human consciousness to act as a mediator that's preventing her human soul from awakening. Thus, in an act of self-preservation, her brain must have shut down, creating a type of self-induced coma. As long as her souls continue battling for dominance, her body will either never wake up from the coma, or her mind will eventually break."

"Then put them all to sleep," Maxim said. "You're human, so I don't know if Needles told you, but we have a drug that—"

"—sedates the animal part of a shifter's psyche to treat those who have lost themselves to their animal souls completely, yes I know," Paul finished. "I've already administered it. That's what has me so worried. Needles told me that as far as anyone knew, it's never been given to a Polyshifter. I gave her the standard dose for an adult female shifter, but there's an enormous possibility that it could make things worse, or not work at all. As far as I'm concerned, both of those outcomes would be equally dangerous. We're going to give her another fMRI in an hour. My hope is that if the drug works and all her animal souls are quieted, then we'll keep giving her the usual dose until her body and mind have recovered enough for her brain to allow her to awaken."

Maxim rubbed at his eyes, feeling all the exhaustion of this endless day start to creep in on him. "Any of the doctors try to stick their nose in where it wasn't wanted?"

"I don't know what your uncle Thomas told them, but they didn't ask too many questions. Kylie also never left my sight, so there was no chance that someone took a blood sample from her on the sly."

"He probably just mentioned that her injuries were Sniffer related," Maxim said. "Shifters will usually avoid anything that has to do with the lions, afraid to inadvertently shine the spotlight on themselves and their loved ones. They were probably relieved to have you take care of everything, even though you're human. These days, a shifter having one human biological parent isn't as rare as it once was. They would never guess the truth."

Paul nodded and then he suddenly fixed Maxim with a narrow stare. "You look like you're a couple of beats away from falling over from exhaustion. I know you said you have some things to tell me, but you also said so yourself earlier that there wasn't anything you could do until morning. You won't be any help to either Kylie or Hunter if you end up collapsing from exhaustion. Go get some sleep, and tomorrow morning after you pick up Ryder from the airport, you can fill us in on everything all at once."

"Ada and I'll stay here all night with Paul," Henry cut in.

"I will, too," Thea said. "We can sleep in turns while we all watch over Kylie."

Maxim frowned. "In that case, I'll just do the same."

Paul shook his head. "If you two are going to be pounding the pavement tomorrow, then you'll need to be better rested than catching a few z's in an uncomfortable chair."

Maxim opened his mouth to protest, but then immediately shut it and nodded. Paul was right.

He turned to Thea and said, "I'll drive you back to Greenwich, but my uncle has plenty of guestrooms if you'd like to stay with us instead."

Thea looked over at Henry and Ada. "If you two are sure, then I'm fine staying with the Clarkes. You can take me to get a change of clothes after we pick up Hunter's brother from the airport in a few hours."

Paul walked over and placed a comforting hand on

Maxim's shoulder. "I'll call if she wakes up," he promised.

Maxim nodded and then turned to gently pick up Kylie's hand, squeezing it affectionately. "I know you'd hate knowing so many people are hovering over you right now, so come back to us soon."

CHAPTER 15

*I*t seemed Maxim had barely closed his eyes when the alarm on his phone began shrieking fit to wake the dead. With a groan, he forced his eyes to open and reached over to tap the "Alarm Off" button on his phone's touchscreen. Five minutes later, a towel draped over his bare shoulder, he was still half-asleep and trudging down the hall to the bathroom.

On the way, he passed Thea's room and paused. The only sounds coming from the room were her heartbeat and the smooth, steady breaths of slumber. Had she forgotten to set her alarm?

He knocked on the door. A few seconds later, he rapped on it again a little harder, but the rhythm of her breathing never once changed. Amused more than anything, Maxim opened the door without bothering to be quiet and entered.

Thea was stretched out on her side beneath the covers, one arm curled adorably over her head and the other pressed against her chest. Her long hair fell more neatly than he would have expected in rivers of reds behind her. For a long moment, he stared down at her, hardly daring to breathe.

She was beautiful.

The clock on the nightstand abruptly began to screech, making Maxim nearly jump clear out of his skin. Without opening her eyes, Thea reached a hand clumsily towards the vicinity of the clock and groped around until she found and pressed the snooze button. She curled her arm against her body and fell still.

Now fully awake, Maxim couldn't help but chuckle. Suddenly, Thea was flying off the bed with a startled hiss, her eyes wild.

Maxim held up his hands. "I didn't mean to startle you."

Thea froze, then after blinking rapidly, she slowly straightened out of her defensive crouch. "I didn't hear you come in," she said hoarsely.

"I noticed," he replied with a grin, studiously avoiding looking too long at her half-dressed state. He had loaned her one of his black t-shirts, and the hem only went down to mid-thigh, leaving her long, pale legs bare. "I even knocked. I thought maybe you forgot to set your alarm."

She pushed her hair over her shoulder and laughed. "I'm of the 'just five more minutes' camp."

He pulled the towel from his shoulder and tossed it to her. "You can use the bath down the hall. I'll use the one downstairs."

As he left the room, he could feel her eyes on his bare back like a physical touch. His tiger stirred within, responding to that deliberate gaze with an interest that was unsettling. It probably wasn't the best idea to enter her room dressed only in estate pants.

Half an hour later, they were on their way to Heathrow with the sun still about a couple of hours from rising. Maxim found that his tiger was still hyper-aware of Thea—her proximity, her scent, her heartbeat and every breath. He felt them to the point of distraction, finding it hard to concentrate on navigating the early morning commuter traffic. That she had decided to wear his t-shirt instead of yesterday's blouse after her bath wasn't helping in the least. He caught himself trying to inhale more of her sweet scent several times over the course of ten minutes.

What made matters worse, Maxim was positive Thea had noticed his growing agitation, if not by the rigidness of his shoulders, then by his scent. Yet, not only did she not call him on it, she went out of her way to keep their conversation lighthearted and cheerful, distracting him, he knew, from the fact that there still had been no change in Kylie's condition when he had called Paul for an update after his shower.

It was because of this that halfway to the airport, he made up his mind to rip off the bandage over the wound in his human soul that was still bleeding and show her what lay beneath.

"You wanted to know what happened in Amarillo," he said during a natural lull in their conversation.

Thea's expression was startled as he turned to look at her briefly before fixing his gaze directly on the road ahead. He had never had to recount any of it. Not to his siblings, not to his parents, no one. He wasn't sure he could do it now, but for Thea, he wanted to at least try. He wanted her to understand why he was so broken, to know how much he appreciated everything she was doing for him but couldn't quite put into words.

"I shouldn't have asked at all," Thea said finally after a long moment of silence, "not about something that's so obviously painful for you to remember."

"I want to tell you."

Out of the corner of his eye, Maxim saw her reach out her hand, pausing inches away from his upper arm before finally curling her fingers around the hard muscle to deliver a gentle squeeze. His eyes flickered over to her face long enough to see her nod, her eyes grave.

He took a deep, calming breath, and slowly began to talk. He told her about Hunter coming to him, frantic with worry over Ryder's disappearance, then of his mate-to-be, Anna, disappearing a few months later. He described the long hours he, Hunter, and his siblings put in for over a year searching in vain for them, and how Hunter and Kylie had found an injured Jack Bray, finally revealing the fate of both Anna and Ryder.

The horror in Thea's eyes had deepened every time his gaze flitted to her face as Maxim described everything Jack had told them about being used as lab rats by the lions in that secret, underground compound just outside Amarillo. He spoke about Kylie's friend, Molly's, abduction by the lions and learning that her missing birth mother was possibly a prisoner in that compound. He told her about the raid and rescue they had planned and executed.

Slow and steady, Maxim managed to keep talking

without pause—until he came to the moment when they had finally found Anna and Molly. It was at that point his voice failed him. He was just unable to force the words past the huge knot of pain, rage, and grief that formed in his throat as his mind was abruptly inundated with the agonizing images of Anna bleeding out on that concrete floor, in the SUV, as well as that last image that had become his perpetual torment of her taking her last breath through an oxygen mask.

He had just enough presence of mind to realize he was on the brink of losing it again and was able to pull over at the first grassy shoulder he could find in that maze of concrete and asphalt large enough for the car before he caused an accident. The instant he put the car in park, Maxim closed his eyes and let his face fall hard onto the steering wheel, gritting his teeth and squeezing the wheel so tightly that his hands started to hurt as he tried his damnedest to push those terrible images from his mind.

Then he felt a familiar warmth as Thea wrapped her arms around him. "I'm sorry. I'm sorry," she murmured into his ear over and over.

For so long, he had always been the one to offer comfort, to be strong, to be the pillar that kept everyone else from crumbling. He didn't know how to handle being on the other end, so although Maxim gave himself utterly to that comfort, to the warmth of being embraced by someone who obviously cared about him, he hated himself for it, for *needing* it.

And still, he didn't cry.

After a while, the rest of the horrible tale came spewing forth hoarsely from his lips as though he was excising a festering wound. "Anna was bleeding out from a miscarriage when we found her. Those bastards had—" He couldn't finish. "She fell into a coma and died a week later. I don't know if she even realized that she had been found."

I don't know if she knew that I was with her in the end...

"We won't let that happen to Kylie *or* Hunter," Thea growled fiercely.

He felt her warmth abruptly leave him and then her hands gripped his face and tugged until he was forced to lift his head from the steering wheel and look at her. Her green eyes sparked with anger.

Her anger called to that barely contained rage within him, bringing his tiger more to the forefront of his being. All traces of his grief were quickly swallowed by the rising wave of fury he had been continuously keeping at bay by keeping his tiger soul as much in the background of his psyche as possible. The snarl that burst from his throat was all tiger, and he felt his canines begin to elongate into the beginnings of fangs.

"No, we won't," Maxim agreed, his voice low and deadly.

With a nod of satisfaction, Thea sat back into her seat and re-buckled her seatbelt. "Now, let's go get Ryder and get to work."

CHAPTER 16

*R*yder found his car before either he or Thea could see him. Maxim had expected the older jaguar to appear without luggage, probably having gone straight to the Riverford airport once he had escaped Sasha and Arthur. Sasha had said that he had been pretty agitated when he left his apartment.

However, when Ryder abruptly opened the passenger door on Maxim's side of the car, making him hiss in surprise, his friend was already pushing one suitcase over the backseat, a carry-on bag strap resting on his shoulder. He also didn't look as rough and exhausted as he should have after an overnight, transatlantic flight.

"I hope you weren't waiting long," Ryder said once he was settled in the backseat. He looked at Thea curiously. "So, you're Kylie's cousin, Thea. I'm Ryder Rivera."

Thea accepted the hand he thrust over the seat for a shake. "It's nice to meet you."

"Sasha was worried about you," Maxim said as he started the car, trying to gauge his state of mind.

The last thing Thea needed to deal with was two shifters on an emotional hair trigger.

Ryder sighed. "Yeah, I know. I've had a whole plane ride to realize how much of a jackass I was about the whole thing. I'll have to apologize to both her and Arthur when we're stateside again. I talked to Paul about an hour ago. Has there been any change in Kylie's condition since?"

Maxim shook his head. "That's where we're headed right now. The last I heard, the drug was ineffective. Paul gave her double the dose about an hour ago. She should've had another brain scan by the time we get there."

"And Hunter?" Ryder asked, his voice tight with sudden tension.

"The lead we were chasing didn't pan out. My uncle's clan has people watching the building just in case, but we have another thread to pull in the Battersea area. As soon as the sun rises, we'll go check it out. We've really stepped in it, Ryder. From everything we uncovered yesterday, what the lions could be doing here is worse than we thought. Hunting out Polyshifters was only the tip of the iceberg. Those bastards are making a bold, more aggressive and dangerous play for London than we've ever seen in any of our southern cities. I'll tell you more about it along with Paul, so I don't have to repeat myself."

"Do you think—" Ryder paused.

Maxim looked back at him in the rearview mirror. He now looked visibly upset.

"Do I think what?" he coaxed.

"Were Kylie and Hunter targeted because of me? I know Hunter denies it all the time, but we both know how much we look alike, especially now that I've regained my muscle mass. Do you think they mistook him for me and that's why they were attacked?"

"I honestly don't know," Maxim replied. "I'm not going to tiptoe around the issue and say no when it's possible. That's why we've been sticking so close together and never going out alone after Amarillo, after all."

"It could also be because they were looking into Henry," Thea interjected, turning to look at Ryder over her shoulder. "It might have made those bloody lions curious about what they were up to. Jaguars around here are rare enough to stick out like a sore thumb." She looked at him pointedly. "You might not want to go anywhere alone just in case."

He nodded. "No chance of that. This is my first time in London. I would get hopelessly lost."

The sun was just peeking over the horizon when they arrived at the tiger clan's clinic. Ryder all but knocked down the door to Kylie's room in his haste to see her. He went straight to her bed and dropped to his knees beside the chair Paul currently occupied. Then he gently took her hand and just peered down at her still form with a stricken expression. She looked the same as she had last night.

"It's working."

Maxim turned his head so sharply to look down at Paul that his neck popped loudly. "It's working?" he repeated dumbly.

Paul smiled and nodded. "She just had a scan about twenty minutes ago. Her neurons are no longer firing so chaotically. Her brain activity looked more like that of a sleeping brain. All we can do now is wait and see. I'll give her another double dose of the drug in twelve hours if she hasn't awakened by then, but I pray it won't come to that." He tilted his head and looked at Maxim with a critical eye. "You look much better. I was worried you would be too worked up to fall asleep though you still look a bit careworn."

"I was out as soon as my head hit the pillow," Maxim admitted sheepishly.

"I expected Ryder to be in much the same condition as you were last night," Paul said, raising an eyebrow at the other man.

Ryder shrugged. "I slept on the plane. I wasn't sure what I would be landing into, so I wanted to be rested and ready." Then he added more contritely, "I'm sorry for all the trouble I gave you yesterday. It was all I could do to keep my jaguar contained when I first heard that Hunter and Kylie were missing, and when you told me about The Chase and Hunter being taken...Kylie in a coma..."

Paul placed a hand comfortingly onto Ryder's shoulder. "The important thing is that you've arrived here safely."

"Where are Henry and Ada?" Thea asked.

"In the cafeteria getting breakfast."

"We should all eat before we head out, too," Maxim said.

"Still going to poke around the Battersea area?" Paul asked.

Lowering his voice to little more than a whisper as a precaution, Maxim quickly filled in both Paul and Ryder on everything they had speculated about in his uncle's study concerning the lions possibly revealing themselves to humans and planting them in companies. He also reiterated their speculation of what had become of the captives taken from Alan's raided clan.

"I asked my uncle to see about getting the building schematics for that condo highrise. In the meantime, Ryder, Thea, and I will snoop around the area, maybe talk to some of the Bengals that live there to hear, first-hand, anything out of the norm they've observed recently."

"I can call Rory and Edwin for an extra pair of eyes and noses," Thea offered.

"Rory and Edwin?" Ryder echoed.

Thea moved closer to Ryder and answered in a barely audible voice, "Polyshifter friends from my clan that have been helping us with surveillance."

"They were the ones who tipped off Thea and me before we were ambushed along Old Street yesterday," Maxim added.

"And you're sure they weren't anywhere in that photo?" Ryder asked worriedly.

Thea nodded. "They said they were in Amsterdam on New Year's Eve that year."

Maxim pulled out his phone and brought up a map app. After entering the address of the building they were targeting in its search, he studied the presented map for a few moments.

"Thea, when you call your friends, have them meet

us at St. Mary's Church. I think it's better if we arrive separately. We can't be sure how good a look those wolves got of them yesterday."

A sudden creak of the bed had both Maxim and Ryder instantly looking over at Kylie. He drew in a sharp breath when he saw her eyelids fluttering.

Paul was instantly leaning closer to the bed, jostling Ryder in the process. "Kylie?"

Kylie's eyelids stopped moving and her once even breathing suddenly became ragged. Then her face twisted up as though she was agitated, but her eyes still didn't open. Paul reached over and grasped her hand. "Kylie, sweetie, it's Paul. Can you open your eyes a bit?"

"Hmm?" she murmured, her eyelids beginning to flutter more insistently this time.

Her fingers curved weakly around Paul's hand. Maxim held his breath as Kylie's legs began to restlessly shift.

"That's it, Sweetie," Paul cooed. "You don't have to move. Just open your eyes a little and look at me."

A few more groans, and finally Kylie managed to crack open her eyes and keep them open. At first, she stared blankly at the ceiling before finally turning her head towards her breathless and anxious audience to stare at them with equal blankness.

Paul gave her hand an affectionate squeeze. "Kylie?"

Her eyes slowly blinked a couple of times before she licked her lips and rasped, "P-Paul? Wha—"

"You're in the hospital," he said gently. "Don't try to move too much. You hit your head pretty hard."

Her face scrunching up into a frown, her eyes slowly moved from Paul to Ryder next to him. "Hun-ter…"

She tried to pick up her other hand as if to reach for him.

The stricken look on Ryder's face was heartbreaking. "No, Kylie, I'm sorry. It's Ryder."

Maxim wasn't sure if anything they were saying was getting through to her. The look in her eyes was still vacant, hazy. The usual vibrant green of her eyes was darkened, lifeless.

He thought Ryder might move out of her line of sight, but his friend didn't move a muscle. He just continued to look down at her with eyes full of pain.

Kylie's eyes began to droop. Maxim thought Paul might speak to her again in order to keep her awake, but he just continued to hold her hand and alternate between studying her face with narrowed eyes and looking over at the machine on the other side of her bed to check the numbers on her vitals.

Paul sighed once her eyes completely closed and her accelerated breathing evened out again. "It's best to let her sleep," he replied to the questioning in all their eyes.

"Frankly, I'm shocked she woke up this quickly. The important thing is that she recognized us." At Ryder's wince, he hastily amended, "Well, almost, but even *I've* mistaken you for Hunter on occasion."

A light knock had sounded at the door before it opened to reveal Henry and Ada, their hands full of white takeout cartons and cups. Paul immediately raised a finger to his lips and gestured towards Kylie with his head.

Ada's lips stretched into a huge smile. "She woke up?" she asked in a stage whisper.

Paul smiled. "Briefly. She was understandably confused and exhausted, so she only managed to say a couple of words. Her pulse and blood pressure are fine, so I'm cautiously optimistic."

"We brought breakfast for everyone," Henry said, as he closed the door. "Eat while I tell you my latest news." As cartons were handed out, he continued, "I got a call while we were in the cafeteria from the last member of my clan who had yet to return my call. He confirmed that he was not present in Parliament Square at the time that New Year's photo was taken. If there are Polyshifters present in that crowd, then they aren't from my clan."

CHAPTER 17

"They're late," Ryder muttered impatiently as they sat in one of the back pews of St. Mary's church waiting for Rory and Edwin as planned.

"Let's just hope they got stuck in traffic and nothing more sinister is delaying them," Thea said. "The nearest car park is only about a twenty-five-minute walk away, but..."

"Let's give them another thirty minutes before you try texting them," Maxim instructed. "I hate to say it, but if their phones are compromised, I don't want the last text you send them to be from this location. This isn't my city, and I haven't the faintest idea how deep the lions have sunk their claws into the various agencies. In a city this large, it's far too easy to disappear."

Thea smirked. "You saw Edwin in action yesterday. Believe me, if someone decided to tangle with them, they wouldn't be taken without causing a spectacle. Too many incidents like The Chase and the humans will start to make a connection and delve deeper."

At Ryder's quizzical look, Maxim explained, "Edwin's sub-clan is the brown bears."

"Handy."

"Makes me wish the bear clan in Riverford wasn't filled with so many short-tempered assholes," Maxim groused. "We could benefit a lot from each other if they weren't so standoffish."

Kylie's phone suddenly vibrated. They all leaned in closer as she raised the screen to eye level. "Good. It's Rory."

"Come to the art college? *Which* art college?" Ryder asked, his eyes narrowing in suspicion.

"The Royal College of Art is nearby," Thea said. "He probably has good reason to be vague, especially after what happened yesterday."

"Does he have a friend that attends?" Maxim asked.

"Not that I know of. However, both Rory and Edwin are taking a different course of study than me, so we don't always hang in the same circles at uni."

"How far is it?"

"It's just up the street, maybe a ten-minute walk."

Maxim stood up. "Then we'll take the long way, go through a few neighborhood streets to the south and then head back north."

Thirty minutes later, they found themselves casually walking up the sidewalk towards the college with dozens of other pedestrians. With all the pizza joints, cafés, and other businesses along both sides of the street, they didn't stick out at all. Even so, Maxim felt as if he was within the sights of a sniper's scope from the moment they stepped out onto the sidewalk along the Battersea Bridge Road. That's why he was surprised to see Rory and Edwin completely out in the open sitting and chatting with a young Indian couple at the bus stop in front of the college.

Neither man acknowledged them as they approached, and the couple gave them a cursory glance as they silently filed past to, after Maxim quickly weighed their options, sit alongside them. The smell of Bengal tiger, intermingled with Siberian and bear, saturated the air all around them. Their sudden request was finally starting to make a little more sense.

Another minute and Rory spoke to them even though he was still facing Edwin. "This is Riya and Ankit. We were on our way to the church from the car park when we ran into Riya. We're both studying engineering, and we've revised together on occasion. She and her family live in a block of flats across from the highrise we're interested in. She was on her way to this bus stop to meet Ankit. He's a student at the college, so they meet here often, see quite a bit of people pass through here—overhear certain interesting conversations..."

"I see," Maxim said, his heart beginning to beat more rapidly in rising excitement.

Riya turned to look at him briefly, her expression grim. "Yesterday around lunchtime, a group of young, human men were waiting for the bus as I arrived," she murmured. "Something about their scent made me instantly want to bare my teeth and growl, so I chose to stand on the other side of the glass divider to wait for Ankit. They were speaking with an American accent, so I thought they might be some of the new people that had recently moved into the area that has my clan so on edge. They really didn't dress or behave like tourists or even university students.

"At first, they were talking in urgent whispers with their heads together, but as their agitation became more and more apparent, their voices started to rise. They were worried about something in their possession, something extremely dangerous they were keeping in their flat and were supposed to deliver tomorrow night to someone they seemed to be really scared of. It wasn't until they started talking about another man who had already been 'shredded' that they mentioned it was, in their words, 'a monster cat.'"

Maxim heard Ryder draw in a sharp breath even as a surge of adrenaline shot through his own system. Had they finally, *finally* caught a genuine break?

"Unfortunately, the bus pulled up, and that was the end of their conversation," Riya finished regretfully.

"Would you be able to point any of them out if you saw them again?" Maxim asked.

She nodded. "I saw one of them just this morning, in fact, as I was leaving my block of flats. He was just walking out onto the pavement from the entrance gate of the building Rory said you were keeping an eye on."

Both Rory and Edwin were now grinning like Cheshire cats.

"Promising, wouldn't you say?" Edwin said.

"More than promising," Maxim agreed, locking eyes with Ryder over Thea's head. "We were planning on infiltrating the building, but if they're planning on moving this so-called 'monster cat,' we just need to wait for them to bring the cat outside and be ready to attack."

"You said they were making their delivery tomorrow night?" Ryder directed at Riya.

"Yes."

"Max, do you think, with your uncle's help, we could gather a group of shifters large enough to surround the entire property?"

"My father and Riya's grandmother are Elders," Ankit cut in. "They've been trying for a long time to get the rest of the clans to look more closely at what's been going on in this area. They've told us of the meeting held yesterday with your uncle. If not for your jaguar friends and the very public spectacle of The Chase, I'm not sure they would've made the matter the priority it is now. I'm sure our clan would be happy to return the favor with a few volunteers, myself included. The sooner we force these lion-kissing gits out of Battersea, the sooner we can walk the bloody streets of our own communities without worrying about being accosted!"

"Thank you," Ryder said, his expression all gratitude.

"Just have your father contact my uncle this evening," Maxim instructed. "Hopefully, we'll have put together a plan of attack to pass along by then."

AN HOUR LATER, Maxim sat in Thomas's living room

with Thea and Milly, listening to Ryder's one-sided conversation with Paul with a relieved smile. It appeared Kylie was awake again and lucid enough to have listened to Paul's recount of how she came to be injured and to ask questions. Ryder was all but bouncing off the walls with nervous energy.

"Yes, he's right here."

Ryder reached across the coffee table and handed his phone to Maxim. "Paul wants to talk to you."

"I'd like your input on this," Paul said. "After Kylie's last brain scan came up normal and she says her shifter side is still sleeping, Henry agrees we shouldn't press our luck in regards to keeping her true nature a secret. He thinks we should take her back to his home to finish her recovery rather than to the Clarke residence where there will likely be Elders and who knows who else coming and going at all hours. I agree."

Thomas was currently off in his study trying to recruit volunteers from as many clans as possible to help tomorrow night in what Maxim hoped would be Hunter's rescue. They were all going to meet here later tonight. He didn't want Kylie to hear any of it in her current condition. Like Ryder, it would be nearly impossible to keep her from wanting to be in the thick of it if the meeting occurred under the same roof as she.

"Yes, I think taking her to Greenwich is best. We'll

probably be planning our rescue well into the night, and she doesn't need to be anywhere near that. Just let me tell my uncle what's what, and we'll be at the clinic within an hour. Right now we can't be too careful. I'd feel better with all of us there to watch for trouble. Don't tell any of the staff that we plan to take her home until we get there."

"All right. We'll be waiting."

Maxim tossed the phone back to Ryder. "Looks like after tonight's meeting, we'll be staying with you this time," he told Thea.

Just under the hour he had promised Paul, the three of them were entering Kylie's hospital room.

"Hey," Kylie greeted with a weak smile as both Maxim and Ryder stepped up to her hospital bed. The upper half of the bed had been elevated until she was more or less sitting up, but her body still rested against the mattress with a heaviness that said she was still too weak to stay sitting up on her own. "Two hot men come running to visit the klutz for just a little bump on the head—every girl should be so lucky."

Maxim snorted. "Yeah, 'bump.' Tell that to the stitches."

He wondered if she even remembered seeing them when she first woke from the coma.

Her eyes focused on Ryder. "Although I should scold

you for coming over here with all the danger, I'm glad you're here, Ryder."

"Good, because I'm not going anywhere," Ryder said firmly.

Then her eyes moved beyond them to fix on Thea, who was standing quietly out of the way beside the door. "I'm so glad you or your friends weren't hurt during that whole mess."

Thea stepped over to the bed. "That was definitely not the way I wanted to meet the cousin I never knew I had," she said wryly.

Kylie sighed. "All those Polyshifters in one place practically guaranteed trouble."

Maxim was waiting for her to ask about Hunter with a kind of dread that made his chest tighten painfully, so when she turned her attention back to him, he couldn't help but stiffen.

"Paul already told me that you still haven't been able to find Hunter," she said quietly. "I know you, Max, so you can stop beating yourself up about it. Hunter got taken, and I got hurt because we were careless. We were so busy looking over our shoulders for an army of Sniffers that we missed the gang of humans in front of us."

"Did those humans say anything to you?" Maxim asked.

She nodded, then winced and raised a hand to the

injured side of her head. "Crap. I forgot moving starts the knives stabbing again."

Maxim felt torn. He knew he shouldn't push Kylie for answers, but at the same time, they needed every bit of information available at this point in the game. This could very well be the *only* chance they had to rescue Hunter if it was indeed his friend those bastards had been whispering about. For all they knew, the lions planned on moving Hunter out of the country. There was also a very huge possibility that they were actually walking into a trap tomorrow night instead of setting one.

However, Kylie took the choice away from him by continuing, "Only one said anything at all. He said their boss wanted to talk to us. They had us surrounded, and their scent made the hair stand up on the back of my neck. I could barely keep from growling. We sure as hell weren't going to wait around to find out why."

"Yeah, we talked to a Bengal tigress that said much the same thing about a group of humans she encountered," Maxim replied. "Makes me wonder if they were the same group."

Kylie's eyes narrowed. "Paul told me about that, too, that they may have given you a lead."

Maxim was relieved. It appeared that Paul didn't tell her everything, just enough to let her know that there was still hope in finding him, that the trail hadn't gone cold. He wasn't so sure if she could handle the pain of yet another loved one seemingly disappearing from the face of the earth like her parents.

"We'll be checking it out tomorrow," Ryder interjected, likely thinking along the same lines as him.

Hearing that, Kylie seemed to wilt. "I can't even sit up on my own," she growled, confirming his earlier suspicions. "I hate being so useless."

"Let all of us do the work for once," Maxim chided firmly. "You already did what you and Hunter set out to do. You found Henry, and as a result, he was able to send a warning to your mother's clan. Let us take care of the rest."

"First things first," Paul chimed in, "let's get you back to Henry and Thea's house. You'll rest better there, and we'll be able to talk more freely, as well."

Maybe it was because Kylie was feeling weaker and more terrible all-around that she merely nodded and allowed Ryder to place her in a wheelchair without even a token protest. Thea volunteered herself to walk beside them to hold Kylie's IV bag while Ryder did the wheeling. For someone who had started out with only an adoptive father and missing biological parents, Kylie certainly had done an excellent job building the loving family she had now.

CRISTINA RAYNE

He would do everything in his power to make sure this new family was never broken. Kylie was his sister in spirit if not in blood. He *would* bring Hunter home to her if he had to turn over every last damned stone or kill every last lion on this earth to do it.

CHAPTER 18

"Max, can I talk to you alone for a moment?" Kylie asked just as everyone was leaving the room to find their beds.

After meeting with the—he was thrilled to see—dozens of shifters that had volunteered for what would hopefully turn out to be a rescue, Maxim, Ryder, and Thea had returned to Greenwich. Although it was only ten o'clock, they figured Kylie would already be asleep. Yet when Ada had met them at the back door, she had informed them that Kylie was still very much awake and stubbornly refusing to sleep until she could talk to them.

"Of course," Maxim agreed instantly even though he felt a little trepidation.

"Come find me afterwards, and I'll show you where

you can sleep," Thea said before closing the door behind her and Ryder.

Kylie chuckled. "Don't look as though I'm about to ream you a new one." She patted the empty space beside her. "Come sit here on the bed with me. This way you won't be able to claim ignorance later. I want to make sure you hear every word I'm about to say. Whether you listen is all on you."

Having absolutely no idea where she was going with this, Maxim did as she asked, now feeling more bewildered than anxious.

"While you and Ryder were off whispering with Paul, Thea and I had a nice chat."

Maxim instantly went rigid. While he was almost one hundred percent sure Thea wouldn't have betrayed his confidence by telling Kylie about his breakdowns, that didn't mean that she wasn't curious about him. Had she asked Kylie about some aspect of his past?

"Don't worry. She didn't go digging for any deep dark secrets. I didn't mean to imply that she had asked anything at all. What I want to talk to you about is something that I've observed—in both of you."

While Maxim was sure she had intended her words to be reassuring, they just made him even more apprehensive. Kylie had always had a *way* of looking at him, seeing through the façade that everyone else usually bought no matter how closely they looked at him. No doubt he had just now given something away he had never intended—and he had a sneaking suspicion he knew what it was.

"I know what you're going to say," Maxim said, deciding to just take the bull by the horns. "It can't happen."

Kylie's eyes widened a bit. "I didn't think you would admit it this quickly, if at all."

"I know you," he said with a small smile. "I've learned by now it's useless to deny anything to you and your preternatural nose."

That same nose wrinkled. "You make me sound like a bloodhound."

"Better than a bloodhound," he corrected.

"Well, Thea told this bloodhound that when this is all over, she wanted to go back to Riverford with us." Kylie made a face. "After some of the things she told me about life in her village, I don't blame her at all. My grandfather sounds like a dictator. Anyway, what I'm trying to say is the opportunity is there. That's *all*. No one but you can decide what your soul needs or what you *can* allow yourself. A year ago, I was in a much much lesser version of the place you're in now, so I wanted to at least give you something to chew on. I realized there was no right or wrong choice. There was only the choice I wanted and the choice I could live with. The choice I ultimately made could have been either of those things, none of those things, or both. To leave or stay? I chose to stay with Hunter because I couldn't live with the regret."

Kylie reached over, took his hands and squeezed them tightly between her own. "I saw the choice you want—at least a potential one. Just remember one of the choices is you don't have to choose at all because you decide there's nothing for you to choose in the first place. The important thing is to just do *something*, whether that something is merely recognizing there's something to consider in the first place and deciding not to."

"You shouldn't be worrying about me right now," Maxim murmured.

"Worrying is fretting about those really dark circles you currently have under your eyes or that you flew across an ocean and are now neck-deep in potential danger because of me. I was simply giving you *advice* out of love, but thanks for the reminder. I'll now be worrying about what you and Ryder were whispering about with Paul all night."

Maxim leaned forward and kissed her on the forehead. "No, you won't because I'll have Paul slip you something in your IV that'll knock you out 'til morning."

"You're terrible," Kylie groused, but she was grinning.

"Get some sleep," Maxim said as he stood up. "We all have a busy day tomorrow."

The house was quiet as he walked down the hall and headed down the stairs instead of seeking Thea out as told. He needed somewhere quiet to think because as much as he hated to admit it, what Kylie had said really got under his skin, and he didn't know if he could handle seeing Thea just yet.

Maxim was relieved to find the living room dark and empty. He sat down on an overstuffed armchair and leaned into the softness with a weary sigh.

He was attracted to Thea.

The admission, even if only to himself within his mind, made his heart thump painfully in sudden anxiety. Agreeing with Kylie was one thing. Admitting it outright somehow made it more real, made it into that "choice" Kylie had been talking about.

It made him wonder if he even deserved to feel that kind of desire at all, much less act on it.

Thea deserves better.

"I 'deserve' nothing."

Maxim hung his head and roughly grabbed at his hair with both hands, tugging viciously. He suddenly had the worst urge to roar until his voice gave out.

What was right and what was wrong? Kylie had said

those were the wrong questions to ask, but he just didn't know how to look at it any other way. He had loved Anna deeply, *still* loved her. Did he have to let go of that love in order to make room in his heart to maybe someday love Thea just as deeply?

He blew out a frustrated breath. No one was asking him to do that, least of all Thea. He paused. Hell, no one was asking him to do anything at all. The only reason why he was running around in circles now was that he was attracted to Thea *and* he wanted to pursue that attraction. He genuinely wanted to see what could be— and that made him feel guiltier than all hell.

He shouldn't *want* to feel excitement again.

He shouldn't want to feel the warmth of another pressed up against his naked skin again.

He shouldn't want to smile and laugh and feel alive again.

He was just supposed to *exist*. That was his atonement. That was his punishment for all those months Anna had suffered, been tortured in unimaginable ways because he hadn't been good enough to find her in time. Not because someone had sentenced him for his failings, but because it was, he suddenly realized, the choice he could live with, the only choice he *could* make and not give over dominance to his tiger soul forever.

Maxim slowly relaxed his fingers from their death-grip on his hair and lowered them to his lap.

Was that still the only choice he could live with?

A creak in the floorboards near the door let him know he was no longer alone. "I told you to come find me."

He nodded without looking at her. "I was thinking."

"I can understand that." Thea reached down and lightly squeezed his shoulder. "You can have the down-stairs guestroom. It's that door on the other side of the—"

She abruptly broke off mid-sentence with a startled gasp as Maxim was suddenly on his feet, towering over her and encircling her face with both hands. He felt a slight rise in the warmth against his fingertips as she flushed a split-second before he lowered his lips down to hers.

A slow but firm caress of his lips against the softness of her own, and the stiffness of surprise instantly melted as Thea opened her mouth to him and pressed her body more firmly against his own. Maxim felt her shiver as he slowly traced her plump, bottom lip with a teasing swipe of his tongue before plunging it within, finding the slick, silkiness of her own tongue waiting and eager.

It wasn't until he felt a jolt that reverberated through both their bodies and a gasp from Thea that Maxim realized he had unconsciously pushed her back into the wall. Although the only things he could hear were the roaring of his blood through his ears and the rapid beating of both their hearts, no doubt slamming her back against the wall had caused a loud thud. The last thing he wanted was for someone to come running and find them furiously grinding against each other sucking face against the living room wall.

With an effort, Maxim pulled away from that luscious mouth just enough to gasp out, "You were saying about that bedroom?"

Thea lowered her hands and slid them sensually down over his shirt until they roughly cupped his ass through his jeans. She gave his lips a playful nip. "Follow me."

After Maxim pulled away from her reluctantly, Thea grabbed his hand and led him out of the living room, past the stairs, and across the dining room to a closed door. She wasted no time in pulling him inside, not bothering with the lights as there was plenty of moonlight coming through a narrow slit in the curtains for their shifter-enhanced eyes.

Maxim paused for a moment as he drew her against his chest to just look at her face. Even in the gloom, her green eyes glittered like polished jewels with excitement and her lips already kiss-swollen and begging to be nibbled and sucked.

His body already burned to be deep inside her, to hear her cry out his name, to feel her wrap herself around him. He had made his choice. Now it was time for Thea to make the choice that was best for *her*.

"You sure about this?" he asked, raising a hand to lightly tease across her cheek with his fingertips. "I honestly don't know if I can give you my heart in the way you may need."

Thea stood up on tiptoes and kissed him softly. "And I'm not asking. I won't ever ask. I enjoy going with the flow. It's fun and exciting to not be able to see what life has in store for you. Just two days ago I never dreamed I would be here, about to have my clothes ripped off by a blond tiger stud from America in Henry's guestroom."

"You like to play rough?"

"Well, we'll just have to see won't we?" she said mischievously, reaching a hand to palm and squeeze his already-hard member through his jeans, making him hiss as the coarse material rubbed against his delicate, naked flesh.

Maxim growled as he reached down to grasp the hem of the pale-blue t-shirt she was wearing and whisked it over her head in one fell swoop, revealing her naked breasts. Her nipples immediately hardened into pebbles in the cool air, and Maxim couldn't resist bending down to lick one of them playfully, making her gasp.

Along with the soft, cotton shorts she was wearing, it was clear that she was dressed for bed. While he would no doubt enjoy teasing and slowly undressing her in the future, for tonight, he couldn't wait to feel the whole of her naked flesh rubbing against his own skin.

He picked her up and tumbled them both onto the bed as she laughed and immediately wiggled until she could wind her legs tightly around his waist, her hair spread out wildly and bright against the lavender duvet. She lifted her face to him for a kiss which he eagerly gave, one of his hands moving to cup and caress a breast that seemed to fit perfectly in his hand while he ground his pelvis against the soft center of her pleasure. Her resulting moan made his lips tingle, and the sound seemed to skirt down his spine straight into his cock, making his hips rock against her groin more insistently to feel more of that delicious friction.

"Not...fair..." Thea panted between kisses.

He felt her tug hard at the hem of the long-sleeved Henley he was wearing, trying to lift it up his body. Maxim gave her one last, hard kiss before he sat up, his knees still straddling her waist, and pulled off his shirt, tossing it over the side of the bed onto the hardwood floor. He then looped his fingers beneath the waistband of her shorts and panties while she lifted her butt off the bed, allowing him to easily slide them down her long legs to join his shirt on the floor.

Now completely naked, his eyes only had time to roam down the creamy-white length of her body appreciatively once before Thea sat up and began unbuttoning and unzipping his jeans, discovering with an exclamation of delight that he wore no underwear when all eight inches of his engorged cock sprang forth eager to play. She wrapped her right hand around it and started to slowly twist and massage up and down its length while her thumb rubbed over the head and her left hand began to caress and knead his scrotum.

Maxim groaned, threading his fingers through her hair to massage her scalp in encouragement as he watched her watching herself pleasure him. However, when her hand stopped and her head lowered to taste him, he pressed a hand gently to her forehead to still her movement despite how badly he wanted to feel that hot mouth close around his hardness.

"Next time," he replied to her quizzical look. "Let me worship your body tonight."

Maxim pushed her onto her back again and slipped one knee between her legs, pressing it teasingly against her clit until she gasped and bucked. An explosion of female pheromones suddenly rocked his senses. However, he was prepared for the onslaught, and he just inhaled deeply and enjoyed the hot arousal that shot through his body and made his head spin. It had been ages since he had allowed himself to savor a scent so sweet and delicious.

Then he lowered his mouth to her right breast and began to suck and gently nip at the sensitive bud until she cried out and reached to press his head down harder. The way Thea was alternating between carding her fingers through his hair and tugging sharply enough to sting in response to a particularly hard suck or bite on her nipple or to the soft skin above her pink areola excited him, making his member twitch and throb, desperate to be caressed again.

However, instead of grinding against her, Maxim moved down from her breasts and began to lick a drawn-out sensual path down her abdomen, pausing to dip his tongue teasingly into her bellybutton. He loved the way it made her squirm and release more of those mouth-watering pheromones.

Then her body tensed with anticipation, and the hand that had been massaging his scalp clenched a handful of his blond strands tightly as he reached her sweet core, red curls damp with her excitement tickling the tip of his nose. Maxim took a moment to inhale the rich scent of her essence before flicking out his tongue and almost delicately licking over her clit.

Thea's spread thighs inadvertently slammed into the side of his head as she cried out and arched up into his mouth, nearly pulling his hair out at the roots. "Maxim!"

Maxim grunted at the sharp pain but didn't slow the vigorous licks and swirls of his tongue over her sensitive button, pleased beyond measure to hear his name shouted in pure ecstasy, making the tiger soul within him purr. She must have had a fist stuffed in her mouth when her first orgasm abruptly began to sing throughout her body because the sharp cry that was wrenched from her throat was oddly muffled. Although his tiger growled at being denied her "roar" of satisfaction, his human side was amused that she was obviously worried about their housemates hearing their intimacy.

He gave a few more firm licks to that little bundle of nerves to enhance the pleasurable spasms rocking her groin. Then Maxim slid up the incredible mix of lean muscles and soft curves of her body, pausing to suck on her nipples briefly again before moving to lick a slow path up her chest and along her neck to her pulse point. He latched onto the skin with a hard suck of his lips at the same time as he finally allowed his body to settle down heavily onto her own, letting her feel a good portion of his weight in a minor show of dominance. He loved the way Thea's thighs automatically tightened against him and how she raised her ass slightly to grind up against his leaking member.

His hips began to grind against her slick folds in firm, prolonged circles that rubbed against her clit and made her writhe and moan and buck her hips until her nails abruptly dug in deep into the muscles of his back just below his shoulders, and her entire body began to spasm in a second climax. He swallowed her cries with a deep, aggressive kiss that attempted to suck the air from her lungs while her legs squeezed his sides harder and his hips continued to thrust against that hot moistness.

Even as Thea was still riding that quivering, pleasurable high, Maxim positioned his cock at her passage, rubbing it back and forth over the opening a couple of times until the head was thoroughly coated with her juices. All the while, he watched her face, flushed and panting, and looking up at him in utter surrender.

Knowing how uncomfortable his girth could be in the beginning, he carefully pushed the head in until the tip met with a slight resistance and she gasped, allowing her to adjust for a few seconds before filling her completely with a single, hard thrust that made her moan. Her channel squeezed him tightly until Maxim thought he might come just from that pressure, alone, but some of that distress must have shown on his face because Thea gripped his shoulders firmly and he felt the tension in her entire body began to relax.

Soon, the pressure engulfing his cock lessened enough that he was able to pull out slightly and thrust back into her scorching warmth more easily. Then he was rocking her body steadily with deep, powerful thrusts that she began to eagerly match with an upward thrust of her hips.

Eyes that had been half-closed and dazed from her earlier pleasure lowered completely as she tilted her head and captured his lips in a slow, sensual kiss that was worlds different from the way they had been devouring each other's lips after her last climax. Maxim could feel the slightly painful but oh-so-delicious-pressure of his own approaching orgasm, but he wanted her to feel that ecstasy again before he let go. He reached down a hand between them and began to massage her clit with a firm, circular motion of a couple of his fingers to give her that extra push.

"Maxim...!" she groaned, her head falling back and exposing her neck to his tongue and teeth as her hands lowered to his ass and began clenching at and caressing the hard muscles aggressively.

Maxim's thrusts sped up at the sound of her voice, his smooth rhythm falling apart as the muscles of her passage began to spasm and tighten with another orgasm. He groaned against her neck as he slammed into that tight warmth with a final thrust that was probably a lot rougher than he had intended and spilled his seed deep within her along waves of intense pleasure that bordered on painful.

He was barely aware that his hips had started to thrust into her again, instinctually trying to milk every ounce of pleasure possible from his still-hardened cock. Thea moaned and wrapped her legs around his thighs, her fingertips gliding up and down the damp skin on his back in teasing encouragement. His hips gradually began to slow as he pressed loving kisses on her neck, then her lips before they stopped altogether and Maxim relaxed almost his full weight onto her body.

Thea's legs slowly slid from around his body until her feet rested flat on the bed with her knees up and pressed against his sides, his upper body wrapped tightly in her arms as though she was loath to release him.

Not that he wanted to be released anytime soon.

For a long moment, the only sounds in the room were their harsh breaths and the racing of two hearts that didn't seem as if they were going to settle down anytime soon. Maxim's thoughts were also quiet, and he was grateful.

He wasn't sure what he should be feeling.

The guilt that he had given in to his desires was there at the edges of his awareness. Maxim knew that the moment he allowed himself to turn his attention to it, it would come crashing down on him like an avalanche, and he wasn't sure how he would react.

Feeling Thea beneath him made that guilt press more insistently against his awareness. She was the one that stood to be hurt the most here. Guilt for wanting another and guilt for hurting Thea because of that guilt. What choice could he live with?

If only it really was that simple.

Maxim tensed his body and rolled them over until Thea was lying snugly on top on his chest within his embrace with a waterfall of red hair tickling his sides. That hair felt heavenly.

She laughed. "My head is spinning."

Maxim raised a hand and began to thread it through her hair lazily. "I would've been disappointed in myself if it wasn't."

Another chuckle. "I don't think there was ever any danger of that." Thea kissed his chest with gentle affection. "You're finally completely relaxed. I'm glad."

Even now she was thinking of him first. Once again, Maxim was torn. He didn't know whether to feel guilty or immensely blessed. He looked down at her lying so sated and peaceful on his chest and felt his heart swell with a gentle affection. Maybe Thea's "go with the flow" philosophy was ultimately the best path forward for both of them.

"And you're still way too lucid," he leered. "I'll just have to try harder next time to make you unable to think at all."

Thea surged up and licked his bottom lip, her eyes glittering wickedly. "I'll look forward to it."

CHAPTER 19

When Thea's phone alarm sounded in the morning, the room was still dark. Maxim blinked drowsily at the groaning redhead squirming on his chest. He figured she was immensely regretting her decision to maintain the status quo and attend her Monday lectures. Since he was to blame for her reduced sleep, it was only fair that he get up with her.

Smiling mischievously, he slid a hand suggestively over the curve of her ass and gave the firm muscle a playful squeeze. "Wake up, sleepy."

"You really don't play fair," Thea muttered, raising her head to glare at him blearily.

He grinned. "You can still change your mind."

She sighed. "No, I can't. We talked about this. The

shifters helping us with the rescue can't see me with you at all or else I can't play my part and keep my Polyshifter heritage a secret. I need to be seen acting normally at uni with my friends, so it'll muddy the waters enough if anyone ever puts two and two together about your 'friend who wishes to remain anonymous.'"

Maxim kissed her forehead. "Then we better get up. Paul's an early bird, so no doubt he's up."

Thea shot up instantly. "I told him this room was where you were sleeping. I don't want him coming in here to get an eyeful. I would never be able to look him in the eyes without blushing again!"

She scrambled off the bed and began hunting for her discarded clothes while Maxim sat up, the sheets pooling in his lap, and watched her with amusement. Despite their late night and vigorous "workout," he felt refreshed. Later he would examine that fact more closely, but for now, he was just going to enjoy and use it to his advantage. Today, he would need to be as sharp and energetic as possible. Hunter's life depended on it, and he would *not* fail another loved one again.

"You're doing it again."

Startled, Maxim focused once again on Thea, who was now dressed in her shorts and t-shirt. "Doing what?"

She walked over to the bed and then bent to give him

a deep kiss, which he eagerly reciprocated. "Worrying," she murmured against his lips.

"I was thinking about Hunter," he replied honestly.

For a split-second, worry also flashed across her eyes, but then her mouth firmed and she said, "We'll snatch him back from those bloody gits. We'll make it happen."

His own eyes hardened. "We will."

After showering—separately—they found Paul, Henry, and Ada sitting in the breakfast nook just off the kitchen.

"Kylie and Ryder are still asleep," Paul said as they sat down at the table. "I don't think Ryder slept well last night, so now that he's actually out, I thought it best to let him sleep a bit longer."

"And Kylie?" Maxim asked.

"I woke her up a couple of times turning the night just to be sure, but I don't think we have to worry about her animal souls fighting for dominance anymore."

"She smelled very strongly of jaguar this morning," Henry added, "so the drug is no longer affecting her."

"We still have several more doses on hand just in case," Paul said, "but I really don't think they'll be needed."

As they were treated to a full English fry-up of eggs fried sunny-side up, bacon, pork sausage, baked beans, broiled tomatoes, and slices of bread fried in bacon drippings courtesy of Ada, Maxim totally expected one of them to bring up the fact that Thea had not slept in her room. However, no one said a word or even acted differently towards them.

Not wanting to add any unnecessary awkwardness into the dynamics, Maxim kept his interactions with Thea on the platonically friendly side only, careful not to think of last night's bed-play at all to avoid inadvertently giving Henry a nose-full of too much information. They would find out soon enough, hopefully when he was better prepared emotionally to deal with the inevitable questions, himself.

Once Kylie woke up, he spent an hour with her, filling her in on the condo highrise he told her he was going to spend all day staking out with Ryder. He felt rotten about the huge lie of omission he was feeding her, but it was more important to keep her here, recovering safely in bed, rather than for her to get involved in a rescue mission that could very well turn out to be a false alarm.

Maxim also studiously avoided bringing up Thea at all. Once this whole mess was over, he would be sure to thank Kylie profusely for opening his eyes to the fact that his life could take another path he truly thought himself incapable of taking.

Then Ryder joined them, and he left his two friends alone for a while to go talk to Paul downstairs in the living room.

"We're about to head out to my uncle's house for one last meeting with all of tonight's players," Maxim said. "I'm sure she knows something's up, but at least she's chosen to play along. If she knew what we were really doing tonight..."

"While this puny human is no match for a shifter's strength, Henry will make sure she doesn't try to run off when my back's turned," Paul assured him grimly.

"Just be ready. If the cat those assholes are moving tonight really is Hunter, there's no telling what condition he'll be in either physically or mentally. We have no way of knowing if the shift was even voluntary or a result of his—psyche breaking." Once again, a vision of that poor coyote shifter they had seen dead in that underground room flashed in his mind's eye, making Maxim's heart clench painfully. "You might have to keep Kylie away from him in the beginning."

"I WENT downstairs looking for you last night."

Maxim's hands jerked on the steering wheel, nearly making him veer off the road. Although his friend's tone was in no way, shape, or form accusative, Maxim still felt a sense of dread as he turned to look at Ryder.

"I cringe to think when exactly that was."

Ryder's lips quirked up. "Don't worry. It was well after all the action. I got as far as your bedroom door before I had to back up in a hurry. Polyshifter pheromones are really something else."

Maxim grimaced. "So I'm learning, but can we talk about this later?"

They were currently on their way to the Battersea area, the last ones scheduled to arrive. Throughout the day, the shifters that had volunteered to help with the ambush had been arriving in separate groups at different times. With the aid of the Bengals that lived in the area, they had been holing up in apartments in the buildings across from and next to the targeted highrise, waiting to trickle out at their appointed time. Others were parked where possible along every potential escape route, prepared to barricade the roads if necessary.

Maxim was leading a group of twenty shifters, including Ryder, that would essentially be the ground troops. Using Thea as their Ace in the hole, his group were the ones who would confront the humans when and if they emerged from the building with anything large enough to contain a jaguar.

He found himself wishing they had at least a few of their bobcat sharpshooter friends, but this wasn't Texas. Guns in London were a bit harder to come by, especially on such short notice, and the few shifters working for law enforcement that had attended their strategy meetings had asked them to refrain from using any guns for reasons they didn't wish to disclose. Henry had thought it was because the clans were currently investigating something big that had to do with the lions, and they didn't want to draw more attention to tonight's rescue in a lion-owned building than was unavoidable. They didn't want the lions to realize just how much the clans were on to their various schemes, especially a scheme as big as this building's occupants were potentially brewing.

"Normally I would've kept my nose out of it entirely," Ryder replied, "but I just wanted to let you know that I know she's as important to you as she is to Kylie. She won't get so much as a scratch."

So in other words, this was just another way he was being protected *yet again* by his friends. Ryder knew, as well as he, that if Maxim lost another person he cared about to death at the hands of the lions, there was no coming back from that. "Maxim" would be gone forever.

Was there anyone even more pathetic than what he had become?

"*None* of us will," Maxim growled, angry at himself.

Riya's apartment complex was eerily quiet when he and Rider stepped out of the car, parked in the slot in the back that Riya had secured for him. A quick glance around at the rest of the parked vehicles showed him that everyone in his group was here and in place. It would all be hand signals from here on out. Almost immediately, Maxim felt eyes on him, and he had to fight the urge to look around for the source. There was no need. He knew exactly what, or *who* was staring down at him.

As they approached the short, iron fence that surrounded the property just a few steps away from the street, Maxim could already see a few of the lynx and tiger shifters that were part of his group sitting on the grass behind the line of bushes planted all along the fence. The bushes and fence were high enough to hide them from view from anyone walking along the public sidewalk on the other side of the fence, but still short enough to be easily vaulted in one leap when the time came.

"Any movement?" Maxim whispered as he sat next to one of the college-aged tiger shifters.

The sun was still visible above the horizon, but it was possible the human lackeys wouldn't wait until nightfall.

The tiger shook his head. *"No one*'s come or gone within the last four hours. It's right eerie."

Maxim and Ryder exchanged glances. "This might not be a bust after all."

Now came the hard part—waiting.

A few of his comrades took turns playing games on their phones to stave off the boredom while the rest kept watch. However, both Maxim and Ryder never took a turn, afraid to miss any little sign that their prey was emerging. Maxim split his time between watching the tops of a couple of nearby trees and the loading area of the building next to the street entrance of the underground parking garage where a plain white van and a navy-blue van with a logo for a furniture store had been parked. The shifters had informed him that it had been there since the first of them had arrived around lunchtime.

It was around midnight when they finally saw a man emerge from the glass doors in the loading area. He walked past the white van and headed towards the back of the blue van parked about ten feet behind the first.

Maxim immediately signaled his group to get to their feet and into a crouched position with an upward wave of his hand. He could feel the nervous energy coming off Ryder in droves as the older man tensed as tight as a bowstring ready to loose an arrow and bared his teeth in a silent growl.

He then signaled Riya, who was watching behind them from the window in her second-floor apartment, with a raised fist. Her role was to text everyone out of his line of sight and waiting along the roads and escape paths that the game was on. Her boyfriend, Ankit, was among those hiding in various key points in the surrounding area ready to stop anyone who might manage to slip through their dragnet on foot.

That was one thing the Elders had been firm on when they had agreed to provide assistance. While rescuing Hunter was the primary objective, they wanted prisoners. It didn't matter that they were humans, not this time. They wanted answers.

His eyes narrowed, Maxim watched as the man opened the double doors at the back of the van and then walked back into the building. They collectively held their breaths as they stared at the door so hard that he wouldn't have been surprised if the glass had shattered. Five minutes passed, then ten, and still, no one emerged. The tension in the air around them was so thick that it was almost tangible.

Then when Maxim thought Ryder might shift and make a break for the doors out of impatience, two men finally emerged, and Maxim's gaze sharpened on them as they proceeded to hold the two doors open. Another breathless minute and another man appeared walking backward through the doors, his hands holding onto the backend of a large, wooden crate sitting on a flatbed with wheels. It was about four feet in height and twice as long as more of it became visible.

Maxim waited, so tense that his entire body started to ache, until the crate was completely outside the building, and two more men stepped out to join the four already outside. Then he raised his hand and gave the air the thumbs up signal.

Between one blink and the next, a large shadow a couple of shades lighter than the surrounding darkness appeared at the tip of one of the trees Maxim had been watching all night. Another blink and it became a dark streak as it dove straight for the group of humans just as they managed to wheel the crate completely out in the open behind the blue van with the opened doors, revealing itself as an enormous bird when its wings abruptly spread out wide.

Maxim lifted both fists into the air in his last silent signal, and his group instantly vaulted the fence, Ryder in the lead, and darted across the thankfully empty street as the shadow bird reached the group and began to attack their heads and faces with its talons. Screams of both shock and pain sounded out into the once still night as Maxim jumped the fence after them, crossing the street in three, powerful strides.

By the time he reached the mayhem, the large bird had already flown off towards Riya's apartment complex. He also didn't have to lift a finger against their human prey. Everyone to a man was on the ground, either moaning or unconscious, with a group of smug shifters busy tying zip ties around their hands.

Ryder was at the crate, prying open the front with his bare hands. Nails popped, and the sound of wood splintering filled the night. More shifters ran over to help, and within seconds, the crate was opened. Maxim completely expected a jaguar to come flying out snarling, but what actually greeted his eyes was the horrible sight of a jaguar lying limp on its side, its fur matted with bright blood in several places.

He didn't need to hear the roar of rage from Ryder to tell him that the unconscious cat was indeed Hunter—he would know that pattern of spots anywhere. And Hunter *was* just unconscious. Maxim could hear his friend's sluggish heartbeat even over the racing beats of everyone else.

The whole attack had probably taken five minutes, tops, but that was already five minutes too many. There was no telling how many or *whose* eyes were currently looking down at them from the multitude of windows above. They needed to get Hunter out of there, quick!

Maxim, thankfully, had planned for this possibility, too. He pulled out his cell phone and called Will. He and Thomas were waiting in a rented van parked at Riya's apartment complex.

"We've got him," Maxim informed his cousin as soon as the call connected. "He's in jaguar form, unconscious and bleeding, so we'll need you to bring the van to the loading zone ASAP!"

CHAPTER 20

*I*t was only when they were well on their way to Greenwich that Thea dared to get up from where she had been lying on the floorboards between the front and second rows of seats in the rented van. She peered over the back of the seat at Maxim and Ryder as they worked feverishly to stop the bleeding from several of Hunter's wounds.

Once they had gotten him loaded into the back of the van, Maxim could easily smell the sickening, chemical smell of the tranquilizer drug used. It was a bit of a relief, all things considered, that Hunter was out cold because of a drug and not because he had been bashed over the head.

"I hope I managed to claw all their eyes out!" Thea

growled as she looked down at Hunter with green eyes blazing in outrage.

Anyone who smelled her now would never guess that the golden eagle that had attacked the humans so viciously and she were one and the same. His eyes fell on her left wrist. Although he had wondered, this was the first time Maxim had seen Thea wear a silver charm bracelet that housed the blood of several species of shifters identical to the one that once belonged to Grace and Kylie now wore.

"Well, if you didn't, then a few others probably did," Maxim replied. "Some of those bastards' faces were so covered in blood that it's hard to say."

Thea's eyes narrowed as she stared at the narrow wound stretching across Hunter's back that Maxim was currently compressing with a large bandage out of the kit Ada had provided. "What caused that do you think?"

"Looks like all of them were done with a knife," Ryder answered through his teeth.

Although his rage had simmered a bit, Maxim had no doubt that the older jaguar was still hair-triggered. They would all have to tread lightly around him for the next couple of hours or so.

"Bloody wankers. I hope he had least cost them a few fingers."

"We won't know for sure until he wakes up, but he could have a few broken bones," Maxim said.

Thea's frown deepened. "We can't let Kylie see him like this."

"I've already called Paul," Will cut in from the front seat. "He said to bring him through the back and put him in the guestroom Maxim slept in last night. Ada will keep Kylie distracted in the meantime."

Maxim winced internally. When they left the room this morning, he had helped Thea change the sheets as well as opening the window wide to air out all the various pheromones and sex-related aromas that had saturated the air. He hoped they had cleared out by now, or *everyone* would soon know about Thea and him, something he still wasn't sure he was ready for.

It was a bit tricky, but they managed to get Hunter out of the van without either Maxim or Ryder having to stop compression on his bleeding wounds. However, before Thea could reach for the door handle, the door swung open of its own accord, and they all froze simultaneously as Kylie filled the doorway, her hand holding the side of her head over the stitches.

Her face was disturbingly blank as her eyes zeroed in on Hunter. Then Kylie stepped aside without a word and beckoned them inside. Within minutes, they had him on the bed in the downstairs guestroom, and Ada and Paul were urging everyone to stand back, taking over for both Ryder and Maxim.

Ryder instantly went to Kylie and wrapped a comforting arm around her waist. "You shouldn't be on your feet, yet," he fretted.

"I'll go get her a chair," Will offered immediately.

Once Kylie was seated, both Will and Thomas offered to wait in the living room as the bedroom was bursting with people.

"We can't do anything about these wounds until he shifts," Paul said. "All of them will need stitches. Any idea what type of drug they used to knock him out?"

"Smells like that new one the lions recently developed," Maxim said. "Although it does have an antidote, neither one is sold on the market, so I'm not sure if we'd even be able to locate any. I'll go ask my uncle to call his Elders. Hopefully, they've got a stockpile. Something tells me they'll be needing it sooner rather than later."

An hour later, Thomas walked into the room with a vial of the antidote. Maxim breathed a sigh of relief. The whole time they had been waiting, Kylie had sat on the bed looking down at Hunter with a haunted expression, running her fingers soothingly through his fur and whispering gently into his ear while Ryder and Paul looked on worriedly. Maxim had desperately wished he could make that look vanish from her eyes. Once again, he had felt so helpless, but there was nothing he could do but sit by her side and hope that his presence offered her some comfort.

"He should revive in ten minutes or so," Thomas said.

When Hunter finally began to stir, Maxim felt as though an eternity had passed even though it really had been around ten to fifteen minutes. He knew well the agony Kylie had likely experienced staring down at his face and willing his eyes to open. At least this story would end differently than his own. He felt his throat tighten at the thought, but he pushed those painful memories away. Now wasn't the time to fall apart again.

He turned his head as he felt Thea grasp his hand and squeeze. He saw the worry and question in her eyes. Instead of pulling his hand away, he threaded their fingers together more securely and offered her a reassuring smile.

A soft chuffing sound drew Maxim's attention back to the bed in enough time to see Hunter lick Kylie's nose. Her laugh was half sob as she pressed her forehead against his and carefully hugged him around the neck.

"You scared the crap out of me!" she scolded. "My heart literally stopped when I saw them shoot you!"

Hunter chuffed again, this time sounding a little stronger, and licked a falling tear from her cheek. Ryder laughed and reached over to ruffle the fur on Hunter's head as though he were petting an overgrown housecat.

"You scared the shit out of me, too, you asshole. That's the last time I let you two go anywhere without me," he threatened.

Maxim walked over to the bed, Thea in tow, and thumped him on the nose. No matter that he was a shifter, it was always odd to see a jaguar roll his eyes at you. "Welcome back."

It was then that Hunter noticed Thea. He tilted his head quizzically before looking pointedly at their intertwined hands.

"This is Thea, Kylie's cousin. We'll tell you all about it later."

"Hi," Thea said, smiling down at him.

"Son," Paul said, drawing Hunter's eyes to him. "You're bleeding pretty badly right now. I need to stitch you up. Can you shift?"

Hunter lowered his head and closed his eyes. He was still for a full minute before he opened them again and shook his head.

Paul frowned. "Are you dizzy?"

He nodded.

"Nauseous?"

Another nod.

"I think that's our cue to leave," Maxim said. "Get

some rest, buddy, and I'll see you when you're not so hairy. We'll talk about everything then."

"I'll stay and help you keep his wounds compressed until he's able to shift," Ryder told Paul.

"Call us if you need anything."

After giving Kylie's shoulder a parting squeeze, Maxim and Thea left the room. "Come on. Let's go tell Thomas, Will, and Henry that Hunter's awake and then hit the sack."

"Together?" Thea asked, raising an eyebrow.

Maxim turned and bent down to kiss her lips softly. He was surprised at how utterly natural it felt to do that.

"I don't think even the humans missed the smell of sex in that room," he said wryly. Then he added more seriously, "And—after the night we've had, I could use a little warmth."

Thea released his hand and moved in to hug him tightly. "Of course."

CHAPTER 21

*E*arly the next morning, it was Ryder that woke them with a knock on Thea's bedroom door.

"Hunter was able to shift about a couple of hours ago," Ryder informed Maxim at the door as Thea came up behind him still looking sleepy-eyed.

They were both still dressed in the clothes from last night, wanting to be ready for anything at a moment's notice.

"He used up all his strength to do it, so he passed out right after. Paul just finished stitching him up and checking for other injuries. Based on all the ugly purple bruises he had across his chest, he's pretty sure that Hunter has a few broken ribs. No head injuries, thank God."

"We'll go down and sit with Kylie and Paul," Maxim

said. "Why don't you try to catch an hour or two of sleep? You look ready to fall over. I'll come get you when Hunter wakes up again."

Ryder ran a hand wearily over his face. "I'll do that, thanks."

When they entered Hunter's room, Maxim was relieved to see Kylie curled up on the bed beneath the blankets asleep next to Hunter. The room had acquired two more wooden chairs during the night besides the one Paul now occupied, and they both quietly moved them closer to Paul.

"They're both doing just fine," Paul whispered.

Maxim looked at Kylie and sighed. "How did she find out?"

"Ada says that they were talking, and in mid-word, Kylie stiffened and announced that she could smell Hunter. She was already staggering out the door before Ada could react. She caught up to Kylie at the stairs but figured it was better to help her down them before she broke her neck than try to force her back into the bedroom as agitated as she was."

Thea nodded. "Not surprising given a Polyshifter's sense of smell is two, sometimes three, times as keen as other shifters."

Maxim turned astonished eyes to her. "Really?"

It was Thea's turn to look surprised. "What, she didn't tell you?"

"You know she's a Returner, right?" Paul asked.

"Yes."

"When she first shifted, she complained about the scents all around her suddenly becoming overwhelming to the point of making her nauseous," Paul explained. "We thought it was just her body adjusting to a new state, and eventually, she wasn't as bothered. It seems you'll have a lot to teach her. We've been flying blind for a long time."

Thea's smile lit up her whole face. "I look forward to it."

Both Kylie and Hunter slept through the morning and lunch. Even Ryder had woken up before Maxim could go fetch him for the meal. Thea had afternoon lectures that she was torn about attending, but in the end, decided to skip them, wanting to hear what Hunter had to say when he awoke.

Hunter was the first to wake, pulling Kylie more snuggly against his body and kissing her sleepily on the forehead. Then his lips brushed up against the thick, coarse threads of her stitches and his eyes flew open completely. It was about then that he realized that they had an audience.

"What are you—" Hunter began hoarsely before

wincing as he had accidentally shifted his body too quickly and disturbed his injured ribs. "No, never mind. I remember everything quite vividly now."

Paul handed him a glass of cold water with a straw, which Hunter accepted gratefully.

Kylie stirred, likely roused by the sound of his voice. "Hmm...Hunter?"

He put the glass down on the nightstand and then planted another kiss on her forehead. "I'm here."

Kylie blinked her eyes blearily at him before they widened, and only Hunter's arms around her prevented her from shooting up in bed. "You're awake!"

"Yeah, and I feel like shit," he replied with a groan. "Those assholes really worked me over."

Maxim leaned forward. "The humans that abducted you?"

Hunter grimaced. "Yeah. Apparently, there's a price on my head."

"What!" Kylie exclaimed.

"It's not just me," he continued gravely. "It's also Maxim, Jack Bray, and an 'unknown blond lioness who is thought to be a Rogue.' Their words. They even shoved a picture in my face. It was an artist's sketch that looked suspiciously like Kylie drawn from the descriptions given by a once-kidnapped geneticist."

Maxim growled. "I knew letting that bastard slip

through our fingers would come back to bite us in the ass. I just never imagined it would be *this* hard."

"Believe it or not, there *is* some good news," Hunter said. "They have no idea why Kylie and I came to London, but they sure as hell were anxious to find out. After beating me did nothing to loosen my lips, the fuckers even *waterboarded* me!"

Kylie turned horrified eyes on him, and Hunter suddenly looked contrite. "They only did it once. That's when I shifted and scared the shit out of them. But the thing is, they were scared because they thought I was about to rip them to shreds—which I was—not about the fact that a man turned into a jaguar."

"Yeah, that's part of the thousand things we uncovered while looking for you that we still have to tell you," Maxim said. "Recruiting and revealing themselves to humans is only a small part of it, one that not even the London clans had an inkling about. In that context and adding the fact that we destroyed one of their super-secret hidden labs of unspeakable horrors, it makes sense that they panicked and went hunting you two in such a spectacular way."

Kylie made a face. "There are videos about it that went viral. Everyone's calling it The Chase. Luckily, they're all shot from far away, so you can't see anyone's faces at all."

Hunter sighed. "Fantastic."

"At least your trip wasn't a total disaster," Maxim said. "You *did* manage to find the right Henry, and as a bonus, get to meet one of Kylie's blood relatives."

A bonus in more ways than one, he thought as he looked at Thea fondly.

"One of those thousand things we have to talk about, I'm sure," Hunter said with a knowing grin. "Was Henry able to deliver a warning to Grace's clan?"

It was Thea who answered. "He sent my grandfather a message yesterday."

"...and the Alpha's finally answered me," Henry abruptly said from the door, instantly drawing all eyes to him. "He's *very* interested in the photo." His gaze landed on Kylie. "He would also very much like to meet his granddaughter. It may take a bit of time to hash out the details, but it appears he will allow you to enter the village."

Kylie's eyes narrowed. "*All* of us? Even Paul?"

Henry sighed. "I suspect that may be the detail that needs to be hashed out the most. I got the impression from the message he sent that he's expecting to meet with only Kylie."

Kylie snorted. "Well, he thought wrong."

"Grandfather is a real hardass," Thea said. "Normally I would say that it's impossible to change his mind once he makes a decision, but this ultimately involves Grace. He's had people searching for her for ages, for ego or out of guilt for causing her to run away and a desire to reconcile, I can't say for sure. That's why if there's a real chance to find her by talking to and/or helping you with your search, he might just agree to anything, especially when word gets out of how you were able to rescue one of the people involved in The Chase from the lions' clutches. He's an Alpha. The thing that he values most of all is strength."

"At any rate, neither of you are going anywhere until you've recovered," Paul said sternly.

Hunter raised a hand to his face and began to run his fingertips gingerly over a bruised cheek. "My whole face feels like it's been run over by a freight train, so you'll get no complaints from me."

"No kidding," Kylie agreed as she raised a hand to touch her own injury. As her fingers brushed her hair aside, she wrinkled her nose in disgust. "Ugh, my hair feels like I used it to mop up an oil spill."

Thea instantly jumped up. "Come on. I'll help you wash it."

Paul also stood up. "You two missed lunch. Hunter especially must be starving after expending all that energy to shift after losing so much blood. There's still plenty of food left over from lunch, so I'll go fix a couple of plates."

"So, you and Thea..." Hunter said with a grin after everyone except Ryder had left the room. "What's going on there?"

Slowly Maxim's lips stretched up into a matching grin. He found that he didn't mind answering that question at all.

"That's what I'm looking forward to finding out."

TEMPTED BY THE—LION?
RIVERFORD SHIFTERS BOOK FIVE

After a harrowing adventure in London, Kylie and family are finally able to meet up with the Alpha of her mother's shifter clan. However, not only does the meeting have an outcome none of them expect, but promising news from Riverford about the potential whereabouts of Kylie's mother has everyone rushing back stateside. Hunter's brother, Ryder, along with several old and new allies are soon dispatched to investigate a genetics research company in Los Angeles where he meets Charlotte, a human geneticist for the LA lion clan that could very well be the key to not only learning the fate of Kylie's parents but also learning the purpose of the lion clan's secret Amarillo compound.

Ryder just needs to sneak a woman he's not sure they can trust out of the city with the whole LA lion clan snapping at their heels all while his jaguar soul is far too interested in mating her. Easy, right?

NOW AVAILABLE!

ABOUT THE AUTHOR

Cristina Rayne is a *New York Times* and *USA Today* best-selling author who lives in West Texas with her crazy cat and about a dozen bookcases full of fantasy worlds and steamy romances. She has a degree in Computer Science which totally qualifies her to write romances. As Fantasy is her first love, she feels if she can inject a little love into the fantastical, along with a few steamy scenes, then all the better. She is the author of the *Elven King*, *The Elven Realms*, *Riverford Shifters*, *Dragon Shifters of Elysia*, *Incarnations of Myth*, *The Vampire Underground* paranormal romance series, and the *Fractured Multiverse* science-fantasy series.

www.cristinarayneauthor.com

facebook.com/CristinaRayneAuthor

twitter.com/CRayneAuthor

amazon.com/author/cristinarayne

goodreads.com/Cristina_Rayne